'*Sell Us the Rope* is original, ad...
I say, except that I wish I had w...

'Stephen May has always bee.. ....ntive, but with *Sell Us The Rope* he has entered a whole new literary realm. A rare achievement.' **Benjamin Myers**

'Stephen May's writing is engaging in this brilliant tale of revolutionary shenanigans in London.'
Suzanne Joinson

'Boldly conceived, precisely imagined, beautifully written.'
Michael Stewart

'Electrically-imagined, immersive and compulsively read-able. Hums with revolutionary fervour, Machiavellianism and sex in turn-of-the-century London.' **Liz Jensen**

'A brilliant and original blend of genres. The book cunningly mixes fiction with non-fiction, yet all its most far-fetched details turn out to be true.' **Marcel Theroux**

'Stephen May is masterful at packing a powerful emotional punch with great subtlety and dark humour. This book really got under my skin.' **Katherine Clements**

'An addictive novel about the juicy aspects of being human: love, betrayal, power and control.' **Lisa Harding**

'In this quietly menacing novel, Stephen May depicts the early stirrings of the monstrous, inhumane machinery of totalitarianism.' **James Robertson**

Stephen May is the author of five novels including *Life! Death! Prizes!* which was shortlisted for the Costa Novel Award and The Guardian Not The Booker Prize. He has been shortlisted for the Wales Book of the Year and is a winner of the Media Wales Reader's Prize. He has also written plays, as well as for television and film. He lives in West Yorkshire.

BY THE SAME AUTHOR

TAG
Life! Death! Prizes!
Wake Up Happy Every Day
Stronger than Skin
We Don't Die of Love

SELL US THE ROPE

STEPHEN MAY

SANDSTONE PRESS

To Nile Spark

First published in Great Britain in 2022 by
Sandstone Press Ltd
PO Box 41
Muir of Ord
IV6 7YX
Scotland

www.sandstonepress.com

Copyright © Stephen May 2022
Editor: K.A. Farrell

ISBN: 978-1-913207-88-5
ISBNe: 978-1-913207-89-2

Sandstone Press is committed to a sustainable future.
This book is made from Forest Stewardship Council ®
certified paper.

Cover design by kid-ethic.com
Typeset by Iolaire, Newtonmore
Printed and bound by CPI Group (UK) Ltd, Croydon, CR0 4YY

One of the blessings of Freedom is that of harbouring unwelcome, or at any rate, unbidden guests. The Russian revolutionaries, forbidden to hold a Conference in Denmark or Sweden are sailing for England, where they will discuss matters without any fear that the Government will think it worthwhile to interfere ... – *The Globe*, London, May 8th 1907

1

How Can Anyone Live Like This?

10th May 1907

Morning of a damp day when the ferry from Esbjerg bumps knuckles with the quay at Harwich. Three men descend the gangplank slowly, carefully. It has been a restless journey. A choppy sea and too much strong Danish beer. Too much singing.

On the glistening quayside now the men from the boat sigh, straighten stiff backs and try to keep their feet on slippery flagstones. They attract the eye, these men. Koba – you know him as Stalin – is small and wiry, his face pockmarked, dark hair dishevelled, eyes burning from beneath a perpetual frown. Stepan Shaumian is taller, more at home in his body, his mouth more generous, more inclined to smile. They could be artists or actors or itinerant musicians. They have that kind of dangerous shimmer.

The third man, Mikhail Tskhakaya, is older, body fleshier and hair greyer, but you can still see a boyish idealist's face beneath the well-trimmed beard and the lecturer's spectacles.

Koba is the most energetic of the three even when not moving. His leg twitches, pulsing to some internal music. His agile, crow-like face stares around impatiently. He slaps the tramp steamer soot from his trousers. Takes it all in: these looming grey warehouses; these chests full of fat pink shrimps; these coils of wet rope. This litter of unattended barrels and boxes. This stench of rotting fish and tar. These listless horses, plodding past the barges and the pleasure steamers. These children giggling at nothing who should be in school.

He hasn't written poetry for years, but he has tried to retain a poet's eye.

Behind them, the porter drops their cases noisily. Clears his throat. They turn and murmur indistinct thanks. Koba pays the man and sees immediately that he has overdone it again. Sees it in the way the surly fellow brightens. A sudden grin transforms his face. The rough verge of his moustache seems to cakewalk on his thin lip. Koba knows he has to stop doing this. The budget is two shillings a day, nowhere near enough to be acting like some millionaire, like some bloody *hertsogi*.

There is the need to say something.

'Har-witch,' he says, flicking the strange syllables from side to side in his mouth. 'Har-witch.'

'Harridge,' Tskhakaya corrects him quickly. 'It's pronounced Harridge.'

Koba scowls. Tskhakaya shouldn't have done that. Koba will have to find a way to put him in his place now. His brow corrugates but he says nothing. Strokes his dark moustache.

Thing about Tskhakaya is that he is too much the teacher, too much in love with his own knowledge, tone-deaf to the feelings of others.

He compounds the error. 'Time for a little stroll through the town,' he says in English.

English! Another little dig. Koba speaks the most basic English of the three of them. He can muddle through, but languages aren't a strength. Not much French either and he didn't even speak Russian until he was nine.

'Let us meander towards the railway terminus. Meander – such a beautiful word, don't you think, Josef?'

This annoys Koba too, the way Tskhakaya won't use the name he has chosen for himself, the name he took from the great hero of the old stories. Koba the *gmiri,* the poor man who showed true nobility by defending the weak against the strong, who robbed the rich to help the poor, the outlaw who brought justice.

Tskhakaya speaks again, in Georgian this time, 'Come on now Comrades! London awaits!'

Such an arse.

The revolutionists walk from the quay to the station, past scuttling citizens who barely glance at them. Places to go, people to see. Fish to buy. Harwich is a place proud to call itself a town of hurry and business.

They walk past the Alma Inn, where a sign proclaims that wholesome pies and other refreshments can be had at short notice; past the British Flag where a former landlady drowned in the cellar as the estuary surged one stormy January; past the Angel, so-called because it was once – not so long ago – the haunt of child prostitutes. They saunter past the spot where last year an abandoned baby was ripped apart by starving street dogs. Every town, however small, has its horrors after all.

They skirt around the knots of men outside the Packett Inn, the Duke of Edinburgh and The Little Eastern.

'England has so many drinking holes,' says Shaumian. 'A nation of drunks.'

They keep their heads down as they pass The Elephant, where the soldiers of the garrison like to meet, and sometimes fight with, the sailors of the naval base.

Koba leads the way, striding ahead. He does not meander.

3

He looks hard at the people around him as he marches on – that poet's eye – but he is uninterested in discussing what he sees.

Of course there is also something that only Koba sees. The shadow that flits from doorway to doorway, always at the very edge of his vision, disappearing if you try and look at it directly. A presence still barely perceptible but growing stronger, more definite, with every passing day.

A smoky third-class train journey. Smuts in their eyes. The smell of cheap coal seeping into the folds of their clothes. Taste of soot in their mouths. Trying to get comfortable on crowded wooden benches, staring silently out of smeared windows as they are rattled through small, flat fields. Cabbages and sugar beet and potatoes. Fat cattle. Thin horses. Sweet tea bought from a cheerful railway worker pushing a cart along the corridor outside the compartments. He wears a stained blue uniform in heavy serge as if he were a military man back from some bitter campaign overseas. He looks the men up and down in an insolent way. He says, 'Up the Workers!' and laughs as he slops his wheat-coloured brew into whitish china cups. He adds milk without asking whether they want it and lurches down the corridor coughing and leaning heavily on his trolley.

Tskhakaya and Shaumian discuss whether this man will be supporting the English railway strike due to start next week. They are inclined to doubt it.

Shaumian asks Koba what he thinks.

Koba stares into his tea cup. 'I think I can't drink this grandmother's piss.'

Ninety minutes later the men stumble into the suffocation that is London. They have heard about the city's wet black fog – everyone has – but the reality is something else again. As Shaumian says, this fog is like gravity, it's like being pressed into the ground by many heavy hands on your head and on your shoulders.

'Like being pressed into shit,' says Koba the poet. 'Like being *drowned* in other peoples' faeces.'

It is true that the cobbles are treacherous with excrement. There are a million horses in London pulling carts, carriages and hansoms. Each one drops many pounds of dung every day. Then there are the cattle swaying gently on their way to market or slaughterhouse, the clinker-blackened sheep, the pigs who, sensing their final destination, squeal and fight in savage protest, the dogs yelping excitedly around the wheels of the carts. All of them urinating and defecating and no one clearing it up.

Here and there in this shallow ocean of manure are spooled little islands of human turds. It makes their stomachs turn. There is no stepping around this filth, either, there is just too much of it for that. And there is absolutely no escaping the smell, which chokes and strangles, leaves you gasping. The whiff of sewage, but also of tanneries, breweries and dyers. Textile mills, leaky tanks of town gas. Decaying offal. Underneath it all the sickly-sweet odour of unwashed human bodies. Every step means feeling your way through a thick noxious soup.

Then there is the noise. The engines and the motors, the clanking orchestras of machinery. The bells of churches and ambulances, the thump of hammer on anvil in the black-smiths' workshops, the hollow rumble of the underground trains beneath your feet.

Human sounds too. The wild jigs of musicians, the bawdy refrains of the ballad singers, the cries of the hawkers and the beggars.

How can anyone live like this? How do they stand it?

The people of London seem unbothered. Maybe they have other more pressing things to worry about. The wide haunted eyes, papery skin and distended bellies of the children suggest that they are just too hungry to notice irrelevancies like stink and uproar. Nothing on their minds except food. As Shaumian says, if you fall down here these mites will be on you like rats or piranha fish, stripping the flesh from your bones with their sharp little teeth in seconds. You'll be finished before anyone has time to pull them off.

From time to time they pass policemen impassively watching the crowds. Even accounting for their tall helmets and heavy capes, it's clear that they are bigger and stronger than most of the people flowing around them.

'Farmers' sons,' says Tskhakaya knowingly. 'Fattened on meat and eggs and brought to the city to defend the property of the bourgeoisie and to intimidate the working class.'

Twenty minutes' walk from Liverpool Street station the men approach the narrow streets of Whitechapel, where the square boxes of the houses become smaller and where the pavements are even dirtier, even more crowded, yet the Georgians begin to feel a little more at ease. They now hear languages more familiar to them than English: Russian, Polish, German, Yiddish, Hungarian, Turkish. A lively choir of almost intelligible words. They begin to see people who look like they do too. Bright-eyed, raven-haired, argumentative people in dark clothes. Men and women who are raucously alive unlike these sickly English wraiths they move among. There are still plenty of pubs but there are also cafes and eating places of all kinds and from all corners of the earth.

The three of them stop to buy gefilte fish from an Armenian street seller. As they eat, Tskhakaya tells them that in these East London rookeries there are 120,000 Jewish refugees from the pogroms, among them many revolutionary Socialists.

'Of course there are also gangsters,' he says. 'Jewish gangs and Slavic gangs, sometimes working together, sometimes engaging in bloody feuds. Boys skilled in the arts of blade and garotte.'

'You hear that, Koba?' says Shaumian. 'Socialists and warring gangsters. A real home from home.'

They must register in the Polish Workers Club. Outside its grey door, watching the delegates arrive are an odd assortment of onlookers: bored men from the London newspapers in more or less serviceable suits and bowler hats, two men from the Okhrana in thick coats, buttoned against the drizzle, and two youngish men from MO5, hiding their own boredom behind the keen stares befitting policemen recently promoted from uniformed duties. A man from the *Daily Mirror* goes to the trouble of taking a picture but he has the casual style of someone who knows it won't be used. This is just the reflexive action of a conscientious employee.

An Okhrana man spits on the ground. He has no interest in blending in. His job is not just to see but to be seen. We're on to you, his presence says. Your studied ordinariness won't save you, your ridiculous aliases won't save you, we see it all, my colleagues and me, we see it all and find it pathetic, frankly. Besides, the best of you work for us.

The men stop. Koba grunts. Then he's off, stepping towards the little gaggle of spectators in that pigeon-toed way he has.

He plants himself in front of the reporter who took the picture. In his tunic and his high boots he has a comic operetta look, an impression strengthened when he pulls himself up to his full two arshini height and flourishes an open palm before him like a messenger on the stage. Like a minor character from Chekov. The reporter, a dumpling-faced man with mild clerical eyes, simply stares back. A silence stretches out between them.

'Koba!' Shaumian hisses, 'Koba! What are you doing?'

Koba says nothing but jerks his hand out further towards the blinking journalist. One of the other reporters laughs.

'I think he wants the snap, Ralph. Maybe it's a souvenir of his trip to England, something for the wife and kiddies.'

'This lot don't do family life, mate,' says a companion. 'All free love and nudism for them.'

'Well, whatever he wants he can bloody whistle,' says the man called Ralph. His face might be gentle but he has a bruiser's voice. A voice roughened in tap-room scuffles.

Koba snaps something in Georgian. The journalists don't speak a word of it, of course they don't, but they understand all right.

'You going to take that, Ralph?' says one. 'You going to be spoken to like that by some Russkie?'

The noises of the street seem to grow quiet. The calls of construction workers – bantering, hectoring, arguing – the creaking and squeaking of the cranes, the bells of the churches, the throb, hum and belch of the steam engines, the buskers, the street preachers, they all recede. The clamour of London reduced to the sound of heavy breaths as two men square up to each other.

Koba is never afraid to start a fight. He is used to winning them, too. As a child he ruled both the school and the streets. If he ever lost an initial struggle he would wait and attack from behind when his opponent was walking away, slamming him into the ground and driving his knee into the boy's chest while his supporters – and there were always many

8

supporters – cheered and clapped. The defeated boy might protest vehemently, might call him a cheat, but it didn't matter: the young Koba would be acknowledged the victor.

These are the tactics he has continued to follow in adulthood. Do what needs to be done. Doesn't matter whether you're hijacking a ship, robbing a bank or fighting over a girl. Go in hard. Use the element of surprise. Give no quarter. Don't allow yourself the luxury of mercy. The one good piece of advice his father gave him: there's no better time to kick a man than when he's down.

Shaumian is at Koba's side now. He soothes the pressmen in English that is broken but warm. He apologises for his impulsive friend, explains as best he can that photographs are sometimes dangerous for them. That they are all on edge. Volatile times in their home country. A rough sea voyage too, it all takes a toll on the nerves. Plus, they are all hungover.

The journalists smile. They can sympathise with that.

'Yes, well,' says the man called Ralph. 'He acts like that again and he'll get a punch in the bone-box. This is England, chum.'

Tskhakaya meanwhile hauls Koba away. 'You'll get us all arrested or beaten up. Or worse. We're here to work, not to perform amateur theatricals on the pavements.'

Koba shakes himself free. Takes a breath, holds it and then exhales noisily. For a moment it's as if he's going to apologise, admit that he acted hastily and in error.

'Let's just get inside,' he says.

2

We Can Dream

At the registration desk, Koba, Shaumian and Tskhakaya line up behind a group of women delegates who are cheerily discussing how to make bombs from household items such as sugar and weedkiller, and how to best protect your clothes while you do it. The most talkative woman has her back to them and they marvel at how her hair is coiled into a red-gold plait that follows her spine to her waist.

'Such an education these Congresses,' says Shaumian, too loudly.

He tells them that a year ago at the 4th Congress in Stockholm a girl from Siberia had taught him how to dislocate the shoulders of an attacker in one simple manoeuvre. It is a story the other men have all heard several times.

'It is something that will come in very useful one day I'm sure,' says Tskhakaya.

The women make frank eye contact and give strong hand-shakes as the men introduce themselves. Not one of them is older than twenty-five and all have an athletic, self-confident manner. They are dressed in clothes that are more flowing and less restrictive than those worn by most of the women they have seen on their way across London.

'Artistic clothes,' whispers Shaumian. 'It is the fashion among the young.'

The women are polite as they give their own names but

they seem unimpressed by the men. Not dismissive, exactly, but cool, brisk and business-like. We are not on holiday, their manner says, we have things to accomplish. Targets, goals. We will not be distracted by anything while we're here, least of all men.

'Where are you from?' says Koba to the girl with the plait, the girl who has given her name as Elli Vuokko. She sighs and in that exhalation is a rebuke, the weary sense that she has to field approaches like this all the time and if he absolutely has to talk to her, can't he do better than this? Can't he show a bit more imagination?

She tells him she is a delegate of the lathe operators from a place called Tampere in Finland.

'I have been to Tampere,' says Koba.

'No one has been to Tampere,' says the woman, her eyebrows arching, her eyes laughing.

'Not only have I been there, it was where I first met Comrade Ulyanov. It was where we began to solve the problem of rebuilding the finances of the party.'

'Ah, the famous delegate from Upper Kama,' she says. Her voice is amused, sardonic, but her expression softens. Any friend and valued colleague of Comrade Ulyanov is obviously a friend and valued colleague of hers.

Comrade Ulyanov. The Mountain Eagle. Lenin.

Now Koba is close to her, close enough to smell the clean, floral scent of her, he can see that she is even younger than the other women, no more than nineteen. Acid blue eyes. Must cause consternation in her local party meetings.

Still, the lathe operators have voted her their delegate when they could have sent a mature man, which argues for a powerful personality as well as striking looks. In Koba's experience, women have to fight twice as hard as men to be heard in meetings, and young women twice as hard again.

Perhaps things are different in Finland from the way they are in Georgia, but surely not that different.

Elli shrugs now, her disconcerting eyes shift away from Koba's to fix on a point on the far wall.

She moves away. 'See you tomorrow, brothers. Early.'

'Yes, such an education,' breathes Shaumian. 'The future is arriving my friends. The future is arriving and it is wearing skirts and knows how to dislocate your shoulders. Strange and exciting times.'

The three men watch the girls swish off to their lodgings until the tired clerk at the desk coughs and sighs that he hasn't got all day and are they signing in or not?

They are given the necessary passwords and handed their allowance and select their new codenames for the week. Koba is Mr Feodor Ivanovich. It is a name he has used before and one he likes. It sounds nondescript and respectable, but it also has a certain swing to it. It was also the name of the Emperor that came after Ivan the Terrible. That appeals to him.

Tskhakaya chooses the name Barsov – The Leopard. Can that really be how this middle-aged schoolteacher sees himself? As a savage cat, lithe and merciless?

Shaumian opts for Ayaks, after the fearless warrior of Greek mythology.

They are given the name of their lodgings: Tower House on Fieldgate Street.

'You're all with me, old chums,' says a declamatory, music-hall voice overflowing with good cheer. 'The world revolution hasn't even reached here yet and they are sending us all to the tower anyway.'

'Litvinov!' Koba breaks into one of his rare grins, a white

flash of blunt square teeth. He is genuinely pleased to see him. They all are. Litvinov is a big man with big appetites. Eager for love, for laughter, for the ordinary madnesses that can be turned into good stories later. A boozer, a brawler and a comedian.

Also the gunrunner for the party. A man renowned for last year's hilarious ruse of pretending to be a procurement officer of the Ecuadoran army. This disguise had resulted in the Bolsheviks being sold weapons by the very forces they intended to use them against. He is a man full of schemes, a man who says yes to every suggestion of an adventure. One of those people others warm to, even those like Koba who are naturally suspicious of charm.

Shaumian produces a flask from an inside pocket and the men pass it around drinking deeply, making a performance of it.

'What is it like, this Tower House?' Shaumian asks. Litvinov has lived in London and is considered an expert on the city and its inhabitants.

Litvinov laughs now. 'Let us be positive, my friend. Let us say only that we will not be costing the party too much money. But maybe those beautifully fierce lady delegates will be billeted there too, hey?'

'We can dream,' says Koba.

Litvinov laughs again, claps him on the shoulder. 'Exactly, my friend, that is what a good revolutionary does – first he dreams the world and then he makes that world. That's what makes us like gods.'

The female delegates are not billeted in the same place as the three Georgians and Litvinov. Stupid to hope to be lucky like that. In any case it is good that the party is not so unchivalrous that it sends its women to Tower House. The lodging house is in a dangerous neighbourhood after all, where the streets are among the worst in London, where most of the houses are in need of repair, with many divided into two-roomed apartments or, like Tower House, turned into cheap lodgings.

The men fall silent and grow watchful as they approach. Even in daylight these streets are gloomy, with toughs in thin jackets standing idle in doorways. Respectable women would be nervous walking to and from here every day. Even those who can dislocate shoulders.

At Tower House they find the doors open onto a canvas screen displaying a notice that a bed costs sixpence a night. In the hallway is a group of blank-faced youths. Nodding at these ill-dressed young men as they pass through the outer door, they find themselves opposite a little window in a recess. Here the manager sits to collect the money for the night's lodging, and keeps the limited range of foodstuffs he sells to the lodgers. Bread. Butterine. Canned fish. Beans. Oatmeal. Potatoes. Gin.

The manager is a wheezy man, with a broad chest and a large grey face. He summons a boy of no more than ten who he introduces as Stan, head cook and bottle-washer.

'Whatever you need, Stan is your man,' he says. 'And I mean absolutely whatever you need, gents. If Stan can't get it for you then it's not worth having. I call him my little fixer.' He winks unpleasantly. Coughs.

Stan says nothing. He simply sniffs and rubs at his nose with the back of a grubby hand. He is a thin boy but tough-looking. Wiry. Sharp-eyed. Snub-nosed. He is dirty and wearing cheap clothes that are too big for him, cuffs turned back on his jacket, the ends of his trouser legs haphazardly turned up, but somehow carrying himself with the dignity of a serious middle-aged man, as if he is an usher in a court or an assistant funeral director.

Following Stan through the second door, they enter a moderate-sized low kitchen, where about twenty men and women are sitting on long wooden benches, or standing round the fire. Half of them are smoking pipes or cheap cigarettes and most of those who aren't are chewing tobacco instead. The air is thick with smoke and the floor slimy with brown expectorant.

Litvinov tries to cheer his companions. He rubs his hands together.

'This isn't so bad,' he says. 'Warm places to sit and think.' He gestures at the plain deal tables and benches around the room.

'Not warm,' says Shaumian. 'Stifling.'

He is not wrong, and the clammy fug is not helped by the fact that all the windows are closed. The smell is even worse in here than in the streets. It is obvious that most of those in the room rarely change their clothes.

'Come on, man,' says Litvinov. 'Let us not be down-hearted. Gloom is a contagious disease you know. It's our duty to fight it, to keep ourselves free of it. And, look, there will be lots of tea at least.' It is true, on the chimney-piece are several tin teapots.

'Yes, but English tea,' says Koba. He makes a face.

'No pleasing some people,' says Litvinov, smiling. Sometimes it seems everything Koba says, however sour, makes Litvinov smile. He finds him endlessly amusing.

Following the spirit of the conversation if not the words, Stan opens a cupboard to reveal the plain plates and cups and saucers which he says are for the free use of the lodgers. He explains that in the basement under their feet is the washing-place and coke cellar, and that on the first floor over the kitchen and a little back room where the manager sleeps, are the beds for couples, and above that a large dormitory for single men. That's where they will be sleeping.

They follow Stan's skinny form as he walks gravely up the stairs and so pass the room where the couples sleep. It costs an extra penny a night to get one of the double beds. It is Shaumian who points out that the privacy of these leaves a lot to be desired. Each couple is divided off by boarding about seven feet high, leaving a considerable space between the top of the partition and the ceiling.

'I am sure the women like it this way,' Tskhakaya says. 'It means they are never quite alone with any of the brutes they are sleeping with. Rescue is always possible even if privacy isn't.'

'The women that end up here are the ones who really need to be able to cripple men,' says Shaumian. 'They are the ones that should learn how to dislocate shoulders. Our female comrades should run classes for their English sisters while they are here.'

There are sixteen beds in the male dormitory, though only two are occupied and neither occupant so much as glances at them as they come in. Hostels, like jails, are the same the world over – curiosity is a dangerous vice in these places. If you want to stay safe you keep yourself to yourself.

These men look like natural victims, look like people who should always make themselves as invisible as possible. Mind you, they also look like they have nothing you'd want to steal. They are just two evil-smelling bundles of rags and bones, two more streaks of pale piss on damp and reeking mattresses.

'I hope our women are in better places than this,' says Shaumian.

'You think about women too much,' says Koba.

'So speaks the recently married man.' Litvinov smiles.

The young women of the Congress are not anywhere like this. They are scattered across London in establishments that vary in quality, but none are in accommodation as rough as Tower House.

At the same moment as the Georgians are surveying their sad lodgings and wondering if they can stand ten days in that place, the representative of the lathe operators of Tampere, Elli Vuokko, is laughing as she plays a noisily competitive card game with Nina Kropin, the delegate of the Kostroma textile workers. They are in Langton House, the bright, clean YWCA in Upper Charlotte Street. The building is new, designed by the eminent architect Beresford Pite in his individual Arts and Crafts manner with banded brick-work. It is named after an unfortunate former Archbishop of Canterbury, Bishop Langton, who died of the plague after only five days in office but was famous for his endowments helping young people develop their natural gifts. No doubt he'd be gratified to know that this monument to his life is modestly comfortable with every little cubicle and bedroom having its own window and electric light – there is a wash-room that smells of lemon, and a workroom containing provision for heating irons for the use of the ninety female boarders.

The drawing room is mainly for reading and music, some-thing that would also have delighted the good Bishop.

Comrade Litvinov is right that gloom is a contagious disease, but he should remember joy is catching too. Fuelled by a rich mutton stew, Elli Vuokko and her new friend are infecting each other with a love of life. They are giddy with the excitement of being young in London, of being part of a movement that will change the world for the better. They catch each other smiling, they laugh at odd moments.

Elli Vuokko shows Nina the umbrella her workmates bought her to ward off the inevitable London showers. In return, Nina shows Elli the revolver she brought over on the ferry.

'Enough wallop to kill an elephant, small enough to fit in your purse.'

Elli's eyes widen. 'You carry this around?'

Nina laughs. It's not like Russia, she tells her. They check nothing here. Think about it: they didn't even need passports to get into the country. Elli feels the weight of the weapon in her hand. The balance and heft. She holds the gun up to the light. Admires the sleek, clean, thoroughly modern look of it.

'Suits you girl,' says Nina.

'Surprisingly comfortable. Snug.'

'I'll tell you what it feels like,' says Nina with a grin. 'It feels like when you hold a man's ball sack in the palm of your hand.'

'I'll take your word for it.'

They both laugh. Everything the other says is droll or clever or wonderfully ridiculous and these high spirits attract looks from other guests. Some, those trying to read improving novels for example, are censorious but most can't help smiling. Good to hear young women laughing.

Neither Elli nor Nina give the men of the Congress any thought at all.

Langton House also features a shop and a restaurant which provides meals for women that are fresh, filling, nourishing and cheap. There is no restaurant in Tower House so Koba and Litvinov leave Shaumian and Tskhakaya guarding their luggage to wander out into the teeming and broken streets to get something to eat.

They find themselves in a chop house, sitting at a bare wooden table on one of four high-backed pews in a low and poorly ventilated room. It smells of cigarette smoke of course, but also of cheap fat and over-cooked vegetables.

'This place reeks like a bloody hospital,' says Litvinov. 'It's probably as dangerous as one too.'

'It'll do,' says Koba and after a few moments, surrounded by merrily boisterous working men, they are prodding at the soggy crusts of steak puddings.

While they eat they talk of the old familiar topics: who should do what in the coming civil wars and the party's constant need for money if those wars are to be won.

'You know, they want to put a final stop to the expropriations?' says Litvinov.

'That again. And who are *They* this time?'

'Same crowd. The bundists of course. And Martov and his cronies obviously.'

'Obviously. Do we care about them?'

'We probably should. Martov especially has a great deal of influence now. He is in the ascendant definitely.'

'And without the money we bring how will the party survive? You can't organise a revolution on the cheap.'

'No need to argue with me, brother. I'm on your side. I guess they think something will turn up.'

'People born rich always think something will turn up because for them something always has. They forget about the need for constant work. They get blasé about planning, about organisation, about the need to be always vigilant, always striving for opportunity.'

Litvinov nods. It is true, brother, but what can you do?

The conversation moves from ideas to personalities and

from there it slides into gossip, who said what to whom and how much they can be relied upon.

They eat quickly and less than half an hour after receiving their meals Litvinov suggests they return to Tower House. Koba demurs. 'You go ahead, my friend. I will sit here and drink another coffee – which is horrible but better than the tea – and record my impressions of England in a letter to my wife.'

'Ah, yes, the lovely Kato. You must miss her – and little Yakov too, of course. How old is he now?'

'Just three months.'

'Three months! I don't know how you can bear to be away from them and here in this place instead.' Litvinov flaps his hand in a way that takes in the dirty tables, the fat and fearless flies and the walls unadorned save for a couple of playbills proclaiming the wonders of a nearby music hall.

'I simply do what has to be done. I simply go where I have to go when I have to go there.'

Koba's voice is cold and his dark eyes have a hard gleam. It is remarkable how quickly Koba can give in to anger, how it can come over him at any time. Litvinov feels sorry for him. It must be an exhausting way to live. It can certainly be tiring to be around. He smiles, claps Koba on the shoulder and asks him to send Kato his love.

After Litvinov has gone, Koba closes his eyes for a moment, suddenly weary. He takes a breath, a swallow of weak and lukewarm coffee and, with a sigh, forces himself to work on his letter for twenty minutes.

Dearest Kato, this city is a machine ... grinds ... crushes ... people here milled and turned until they are less than human ... The words don't come easily and they don't ring true in any case. He tries again: *Dearest Kato, how is Yakov, does he smile yet? Is he becoming his own little person ...*

It's no good. He rises, leaving a small pile of change on the counter. That has to be enough.

He has only moved a few paces from the eating house when a couple step out of the grey smudge of evening shadow. A man and a woman who are neither old nor young, neither smart nor shabby. You can't assess their class very easily. She is perhaps a Lady Correspondent for one of the popular newspapers, or maybe she is the authoress of romance novels, with a small but devoted following among the users of circulating libraries. She has the air of someone whose mind is on other things, that she isn't quite here.

Maybe he is a theatrical agent, with a harem of actresses hoping he'll get them on the serious stages. There is a hint of something Bohemian about them. Something not quite English in the way they walk and the way they wear their clothes and hair. Something European. Some flamboyance.

Perhaps it is just that their clothes are clean.

This suspicion that they aren't English is confirmed when the man addresses Koba in precise educated Russian.

'Excuse me, Sir, we are looking for places to eat while staying in London and wondered if you'd recommend the establishment you have just left?'

Koba has been expecting something like this. Here it comes, he thinks. Orders, instructions, forceful reminders of who is in charge.

'We have had nothing but bad luck with our choices of restaurant,' says the lady. Her voice is soft but clear enough and her Russian is accented. Estonian he thinks. Or Lett. A hint of cold Baltic seas anyway.

'But we couldn't help noticing that you left a substantial

gratuity which suggested that this was a most satisfactory place.' Koba knows the stranger is mocking him somehow though his face maintains a blandly pleasant expression.

'It's all right I suppose,' says Koba. 'Though there are nicer places.' He has coarsened his own Russian, made his accent brusque and rough.

'Oh?' says the lady. 'Where for instance?'

'Kettner's in Rommilly Street, for instance. The *Pall Mall Gazette* rates it highly.'

If the Okhrana want to boss him about then they are going to pay properly for the privilege. His time and conversation are worth more than the price of a meal in a filthy pie-shop.

The lady turns to her companion. 'Shall we eat there tomorrow then? At about 9pm? After most other diners have gone home and we can hear ourselves think?'

'Yes, Kettner's. 9pm, my love. Tomorrow. We'll dine there. Seems like a good plan. If we like it we can base ourselves there for the rest of our stay. We really have had enough of disappointment.'

Koba isn't fooled by this *my love* business. They don't look like a married couple. They look like a couple trying too hard to seem married. They look like what they clearly are: work colleagues.

'I should warn you,' says Koba now. 'Prices at Kettner's are high and no change is given.'

The man smirks, first at the lady and then at Koba. 'Well, perhaps the high prices will keep away these vicious revolutionaries we have been hearing about. In any case, thank you, Sir. You have been most helpful. Oh, and in case you ever need anything from us.'

He holds out a card. Koba keeps his eyes on those of the man while he waits a careful moment before he takes it. A tiny reluctance like this is useful. It can help establish a psychological dominance that might pay off later. He pockets the card without reading it. The men shake hands, bow to each other.

The lady nods as he takes her hand, gripping it firmly enough that he sees the shade of a wince cross her face. Her skin is the colour of sand, he thinks. The colour of summer. He has given her enough of a squeeze to ensure her body remembers him for a while.

The couple turn and are soon lost amid the crowd. Anyone overhearing would have assumed it was genteel-poor visitors to London making small talk. Even Russian speakers would have thought it was an ordinary exchange. Awkward, perhaps, but innocent. A group of homesick emigres swapping basic survival tips in order to avoid being crushed in the maw of the city. Comparing tactics for avoiding food poisoning at the very least.

But nobody has overheard. Not casually, anyway. Not by accident. You can be pretty sure of that. This is something visitors learn very quickly: London is a senseless city. It sees nothing, hears nothing, tramples everything. Keeps moving forward, heedless. Remorseless.

Dearest Kato, London is a machine . . .

He takes the card from his pocket. Dr and Mrs Bunin, resident at the Three Nuns Hotel, Aldgate High Street.

Three nuns. Name like that, it's almost certainly a brothel.

All the beds in the dormitory are taken now and sleep proves elusive, driven away by the din destitute men make when they lie down in groups. Whimpering, sighing, groaning, snoring and farting. All the wheezing. All the coughing. A man is driven from his bed by sudden cramp. He hops and hollers, holding his calf. Someone throws a boot at him.

Sometimes a kind of almost-silence settles in the room for a moment before being dispelled by a choking fit. Or by the lamentations of a dreaming boarder crying out for his mother, his sweetheart, his child.

Meanwhile from the double beds on the floor below come the unmistakeable rhythmic gasps from the men who have paid a few pence extra to bring a woman to one of the cubicles. The beds creak, headboards knock against the thin partitions. Some of the women try to shorten proceedings by urging the men on like jockeys at a horse race. In the dormitory of the single men there is applause as if they are spectators at that same race.

'Get in there, my son,' someone says.

Some of the men put on feminine voices and lewdly imitate the encouragements of the women below.

'Come on big boy. Do it. Do it.'

'Harder. Harder. Harder.'

'Hey, it's extra if you want to do that.'

Such comedy. Such high jinks. Better than the music hall. There is sniggering. There is sordid mockery of the ancient rituals and sweet caresses of conjugal love. One man simply howls like a wolf. Someone slaps him. He yelps once, curses and is silent.

After some minutes the final couple shudder to a finish and now all they hear is laughter, from women as well as from men, because sometimes the search for that kind of comfort is a shared struggle. Ridiculous of course, but it can help.

There is also soft weeping. And that comes from the men as well as from women too, because sometimes both sexes discover that unfeeling company can make sorrow worse and burdens heavier. Sometimes it really doesn't help.

If you manage to get used to the noises from inside Tower

24

House then you are kept awake by the discordant music coming from outside in the streets. Glass smashing. A ship sounds its foghorn on the Thames, a train blows a whistle, there are rifle shots from somewhere not too far away. Some wordless shrieking.

Probably an animal, but it might also be a child.

Koba sleeps a little but when he does the old dream comes to him. The one featuring the public hanging all those years ago of the man whose piggy face so much resembles that of his father. He wakes shaking and sweating. Grasping at consciousness just as the body convulses at the end of the thick and knotty rope.

Just before dawn Koba opens his eyes to find a grey shape at the side of the bed, a bony hand clawing beneath his flat and sweat-stained pillow. Koba shoots a hand out towards the rummaging silhouette – not so much a shadow as a dark stain – and seizes one of his fellow inmates by the shirt collar. It's one of the two men who had occupied the room when the Georgians arrived.

Koba drags the prowler over the bed – there is no resistance – pushes him to the floor and drives his fist into his face.

Again.

Again.

Again. Sickening crunch of knuckles on cheek, on eye socket, on nose.

The other noises in the room stop. No more wheezing or coughing or snoring. No more farting or groaning. There is only this smack of bone on bone.

In this moment, for Koba, the thief is not just a thief: he is Tower House itself. He is London with its stink and its shit. He is the Okhrana with their sly way of reminding him who is holding the reins of his life. He is the party and the way they ignore him, the way they prefer lesser men over him. He is Capital. He is every parasite on the body of the working class. He is all the schoolboys who mocked his lack of height, or insinuated that he was the bastard child of the priest – how else would the son of a drunken shoemaker have been accepted for the seminary?

This thief is also every lad from the streets who has pretended fear at the sight of Koba's fused toes or has mocked the way one arm is shorter than the other.

Of course the thief is also Koba's dead father sneaking nightly into his dreams, depriving him of rest.

No one among the vagrants in the dormitory tries to save their compatriot. No manager comes pounding up the stairs to investigate the sounds of violence. It is left to Shaumian, Litvinov and Tskhakaya to pull Koba away.

'Enough, Comrade,' says Litvinov, his voice is gentle. It is the voice you might use to an uncooperative and anxious horse.

Koba rises to his feet. He is exhausted. He has nothing left. He kicks the prone and moaning body of the thief, but it is just for show now. The murderous lust to smash his fist into the ratty face of the man on the floor is gone.

The thief comes to his knees by slow inches.

'I'll have the Law on you,' he lisps the words through blood and broken teeth.

'No, you won't, Nate,' says a child's voice from somewhere in the dark. 'You'll piss off. You had it coming.'

Stan. Still in the oversized clothes of earlier in the day but radiating authority. This is his world. He is the Law here.

He apologises for the behaviour of the thief and asks the Revolutionists if they want anything.

Shaumian sighs saying, 'It's not even been twenty-four hours since we came to this bloody country. It's going to be a long conference.'

Koba leans down to look Stan in the eye, grasps his shoulder – so frail, like a bird's wing – and growls in English, 'New rooms. Before tonight.'

3

Something Every Woman Should Know

An hour before the Congress opens, the women are training. The chairs are folded and stacked against the walls in the main hall of the Brotherhood Church to allow forty-five minutes of calisthenics and ju-jitsu instruction before the main proceedings begin. The women of the party have the option to do this every day.

No men allowed. They can't even watch. This morning a red-faced Shaumian was turned away at the door while his compatriots smirked.

The instructor is a Mrs Edith Garrud. She is less than five feet tall but her presence fills the large, austere room. She is already semi-famous as an advocate for physical fitness and self-defence. Among her other clients are the Women's Social and Political Union. It is thanks to her that several burly policemen have suffered humiliation in their attempts to arrest suffragettes, have found themselves flat on bruised backs in Westminster gutters as women trained in the Garrud methods used their own weight against them.

In this initial session, Mrs Garrud spends the first half of the class explaining how to fall properly. Over and over, her students tumble onto thick mats until it becomes almost meditative, the percussion and bounce of it inducing a sort of hypnosis.

'This is something every woman should know!' she shouts in English over the grunts and gasps of the thirty or so delegates who prioritised physical fitness over an extra hour in bed.

Elli Vuokko has never done any self-defence training before and she quickly discovers that she is not a natural. Her body feels stiff and awkward and despite the fact she is, on Nina's advice, wearing her loosest garments, her clothes still manage to get in the way, subverting her best efforts.

The exercise also hurts. Pain in her shoulder, pain in her hip. When she mentions this – quietly – to Mrs Garrud, the instructor barks that pain is just weakness leaving the body.

Despite this, after a while Elli begins to enjoy herself. She hasn't been this active since she was a girl playing *kykka* in the fields around her home, and she finds herself glowing with pleasure when Edith praises the way she begins to master some of the simple throws.

Twenty minutes in, she feels flooded with well-being and is grateful for Nina nagging her into coming. For the way she had practically dragged her out of bed. For the way her roommate had simply laughed at Elli's protests as she had chivvied her along.

The moves continue to get easier. By the end of the class she can fall into an elegant roll and be back on her feet in a fighting stance in one more or less fluent movement. Her plait begins to come loose, but she finds she doesn't mind.

Someone who is less grateful for the instructor's efforts is the small, dark woman with the heart-shaped face and the fashionable hairstyle working out next to her. Her face is vivid scarlet with the effort of it. This woman keeps up a constant string of complaints in a variety of languages. English, Polish, Russian, German, French, she curses fluently in them all. Sometimes it is under her breath, but more often her complaints are audible to the whole room.

Mrs Garrud ignores her, but Elli can see it costs her to do so. Sees it in the furrowed brow, in the pursed lips, in the tense set of her shoulders. Mrs Garrud isn't used to complaints and she doesn't respect this woman. Sees her as a nuisance, finds her a rebarbative influence on the class, someone intent on disrupting its flow. She doesn't know who this woman is and doesn't care to find out.

Elli Vuokko knows who this woman is. Everyone except their trainer does. This is the famous Doctor Rosa Luxemburg. The woman who wrote *Reform or Revolution* while in her early twenties, the woman whose colour and vivacity dazzles among the monotone voices and dark suits of the men at every significant gathering of progressives. A woman whose speeches and articles can inspire factory workers and students alike. She is an example of what is possible. Rosa Luxemburg rejects the crushed life assigned to her sex and she lives as if she were already free. She excites people and she frightens people. And in conferences like this one she is a voice arguing for the party to embrace direct action wherever it can. For it to actually do things, to get involved.

She is also, it appears, someone less desirous of physical activity in real life than she is in her politics. It is surprising she is here actually – she has a chronic problem with her hip – but perhaps she wants to show visible support for any initiatives that help the women of the party.

Rosa Luxemburg is not so great at the throws and falls Edith Garrud teaches, but she's an adroit whinger, an adept and polyglot complainer. An activist wherever she is and in whatever she's doing. A thorn in the side of any authority figure. And, experienced provocateur that she is, she knows the value of persistence too. Eventually she manages to poke out a response from the instructor.

It happens when she struggles up from a pose Mrs Garrud calls high plank, saying, 'I can do this, but not wearing this ridiculous fucking outfit!'

She has not chosen the loose clothing of most of the younger women in this group. Her dress is of the plain, heavy, practical type perfect for a working day in the unheated university lecture halls and libraries where she usually spends her time. It is altogether too much for working on martial arts moves.

The air inside the church grows viscous. The entire group seems to be holding its breath. These two women might be small, but they are both fierce. A collision between Rosa Luxemburg and Edith Garrud seems like it might be a clash of titans, however tiny they are. The woman who argued with Engels, who is unintimidated by the intellectual bullies of the Socialist Movement, taking on the woman who once unhorsed a lieutenant of the yeomanry with a shoulder twitched and a wrist flicked at exactly the right time.

Elli Vuokko laughs. It's a nervous reaction; she often does this at moments that are strained and difficult.

Mrs Garrud shoots her a look. Elli can feel heat rushing to her face, but Edith Garrud has returned her attention to the complainant.

'When the riots start these will be the clothes you'll be wearing my dear,' she says, tartly. 'You're hardly going to be on the barricades in a singlet and shorts.'

Rosa is pleased to have got a reaction. Elli can see she feels that she has already scored a point.

Her reply is almost triumphant. 'When I'm fighting I will

be wearing fighting clothes. When there is killing to be done I will be clad in the outfit that gives me the freedom to do it!'

When she's not cursing under her breath, a lot of what Rosa says sounds like the shouted last line of a call to arms. The climax of a fiery speech urging the people out to confront their masters.

Elli finds it both inspiring and tiring simultaneously.

Mrs Garrud backs off from continuing the confrontation, retreats into addressing the whole room with her most comforting mantra. 'Pain is just weakness leaving the body!'

'That's not true. Pain is weakness arriving in the body surely?'

Elli hadn't meant to speak, but it appears she has anyway. She is mortified, but there's no way back. Under Mrs Garrud's hawk-like stare she finds herself giggling.

Rosa turns to her, gives her a wide warm smile, switches from English to Russian.

'Careful, sister, you don't want to get in the teacher's bad books by supporting the class rebel.'

Mrs Garrud sighs. 'English only in my class, if you please.'

'We will speak more later,' says Rosa. 'I feel we should be friends.'

4

A Decent Result

The 5th Congress of the Russian Social Democratic and Labour Party opens with singing. Three hundred voices rise in a bruised lament for the fallen.

The unrest that began two years ago has seen hundreds shot down in the streets by government soldiers, others suffering judicial murder after hurried trials. Thousands of ordinary citizens have been injured and thousands more still imprisoned or in exile. No surprise then that this is a song full of blood.

In a room of fine singers, Koba is among the best of them all. In the wounded intervals of his baritone you can hear the whole history of workers' defiance. Listening to the hurt in the music you can't fail to be transported to the gravesides of the martyrs.

Koba himself isn't thinking of those killed in the struggle. Instead his mind is full of the long day of debate and intrigue ahead of him. A day where some alliances must be formed or cemented, and others discarded.

He is braced for public and vocal ingratitude for his role in the ongoing expropriations. He had once been applauded for these bank robberies, taking money from the ruling class and using it to support the overthrow of that same class. Now, somehow, that strategy is cause for disapproval. Possible disgrace, even. They had tried to put a stop to it in

Stockholm – well, he had won the argument then and would win it again. He goes over the names in his head, those he should be seen with and those he should avoid.

Koba closes his eyes for a moment as the song ends, the last notes curving high into a silence that leaves the air trembling. When he opens them again it is to look for delegates he knows. Kalinin is there, of course, and Vorovsky from Odessa. Look, there is the bundist Abramovitch and just down from him there is the lean figure of Martov, leader of the Mensheviks, smiling benignly as always. A man confident he is among friends. Next to him is his sister Lydia Dan and her husband Fyodor.

Koba's mouth twists as he remembers Lydia saying that the greatest enemies of the people are economists. It is a phrase he has tucked away for his own use.

His eye rests on the slender shoulders of Elli Vuokko. She is standing with other women delegates a few rows in front of him. He marvels again at that long plait and wonders how long it took her to do her hair. He imagines her brushing it out at a dressing table in a spartan but clean room last night – a night which will not have been like his. Her night will have been peaceful. A bit of earnest talk with her solitary roommate about the aims and objectives of the party, then a dreamless sleep before she rises before dawn to braid that plait. Did she manage it on her own or did her roommate also wake early in order to help?

He wonders what kind of breakfast she'd had. He is sure it would have been better than the two thin slices of bread washed down with weak tea that Stan gave them in Tower House.

At that moment she turns around. Their eyes meet. It's as if she knows that he has been thinking about her, wondering about her. She grins, winks.

He feels himself blushing. He never blushes. He hasn't blushed since he was eleven! Has she noticed?

It seems to him that her smile grows wider before she turns to face the front again. Koba breathes out slowly. He frowns. Feels the heat in his face subside.

His eye moves on. There is the young hothead Mikhail Frunze from Pishpek. There is Bogdanov, the ridiculous writer of scientific romances from Solocko, head up, shoulders back, trying to look famous while next to him is Maxim Gorky, a proper writer who is trying equally hard to look anonymous.

There is Gorky's glamorous partner, the actress Maria Andreyeva. There is the rich-kid publisher Leo Jogiches and next to him his companion, Rosa Luxemburg, the irritatingly influential theorist of permanent revolution. Koba notes how grim-faced and tense they both are; how, despite the fact of there being many delegates squeezed into each row, they manage to leave a gap between them. The way their bodies are noticeably angled away from each other.

There is trouble there. Maybe the prison sentences of last year had had effects on their relationship? Jogiches had only served eight months, but for some people even a week can break them. Prison can do to the spirit what water ingress does to a shoe. Doesn't matter how good the leather, or how nicely it fits or how stylish it looks with a suit, if it lets in water it is useless. In the same way, a revolutionary who cannot survive prison with his determination to continue the struggle intact is like that broken shoe: he must be thrown away and replaced.

After the singing, there are words of welcome from their host, John Bruce Wallace, who describes himself as the 'sort of' minister of the Brotherhood Church. This strange looking fellow – he has the build of a bare-knuckle pugilist, but the dreamy, faraway look of the true mystic – expounds at some convoluted length in English on the links between the Christ of the Sermon on the Mount and the people gathered in his building. The delegates listen politely to words that not even the English speakers among them can make much sense of, and there is just the briefest round of applause when he steps down from the pulpit.

The delegates are more attentive when Comrade Plekhanov opens the Congress proper with his speech urging the importance of making agreements when necessary with the progressive elements of bourgeois society. There is some murmuring at this, a rustle spreading through the assembly, a kind of whisper like the sound of a breeze through long grass, but whether it is an approving breeze or a dissenting one is hard to tell.

The first real arguments of the Congress begin with deciding who has the right to be in the room. Martov and many of his supporters are adamant that Koba and the other Georgians not just be barred from voting, but banned from the hall itself. Who do they represent? Who has chosen them? Were they elected in a vote by a quorum of party members? Was the Georgian party even properly constituted?

The arguments go on for what seems like hours. Koba doesn't speak in his own defence. Let others score points with Marxist theory or stir emotion with fine phrases.

After a while, he doesn't even bother to try and follow the proceedings, lets his mind drift, only coming back to the Brotherhood Church when an especially fierce burst of applause, so sudden and so loud it's like gunfire, tells him something is actually being decided.

'A decent result,' whispers Shaumian on his right.

'At least we'll have ringside seats,' mutters Tskhakaya on his left.

It seems that a powerful intervention by Comrade Ulyanov has secured for the Georgians the status of non-voting observers, saving them from the ignominy of expulsion from the hall altogether which is what the more hard-line Mensheviks had sought.

Sometimes to lose by a little when you are expected to lose by a lot is a kind of victory.

'Now we've done fighting about credentials we can get on with some real business,' says Tskhakaya. 'Arguments about the agenda next.'

He rubs his hands together. He really seems to enjoy this stuff.

'Must be time for lunch soon,' interrupts Litvinov. 'I'm ravenous. Man cannot be expected to get through this on two slices of bread and butterine alone. And what the hell is butterine anyway?'

Lunch when it comes is a simple vegetable soup, but Litvinov is so interested in the question of what is meant by butterine that he repeats it to the room at large when they all sit down to eat.

Elli Vuokko says, 'Beef fat and cottonseed oil, mainly.'

It turns out that this leader of the skilled lathe operators of Tampere, this slip of a girl who has already made fierce Koba blush with her bold smile, is also something of an expert on the processes of making denatured foodstuffs.

'Finland is an agrarian economy,' she explains with a smile. 'We are as concerned in the battles between producers of dairy products and their industrial replacements, as we are in the struggle between landlords and tenants, or between policemen and striking workers for that matter.'

'What about the struggle between men and women? Are you just as interested in that?' asks Litvinov. Koba sees how his eyes glimmer mischievously. Litvinov's famous appetite revealing itself again.

Elli's smile widens. Koba notes her strong teeth. This is not a woman who has grown up in poverty. Not a child of the bourgeoisie maybe, but nevertheless someone confident that there would always be meat, milk, cheese, eggs. That she would never be really hungry.

'There is no need for conflict between men and women,' she says. 'The war is always between rich and poor. Between those with power and those without. Between those who fight for progress and those who hold it back. Sex has nothing to do with it.'

She reminds them that in March women had been able to vote in elections to the Finnish Diet for the first time yet many had chosen to support the old order against progressive forces. They had sided with the Tsar who wanted to keep them in their place against Socialists who wanted to free them from domestic slavery. It had been a frustrating time for women like her.

'Finland's parliament is useless no matter how many women or proletarian representatives it has,' says Koba. 'The Diet is a house of paper. One strong gust of wind, one fart from the authorities, and it's gone. No power. No teeth.'

A soft voice behind him. 'Flirting again, Koba?'

He turns to face Julius Martov who is smiling broadly behind the fastidious black beard and round wire-rimmed spectacles that proclaim him to be an intellectual. 'You're incorrigible. And you with a teenage bride and new baby waiting for you back in Georgia,' he pauses and frowns as he takes in Koba's sudden scowl. 'Relax, Comrade.

Apologies. You must forgive me. You know facetiousness is a bad habit of mine. It often gets me into trouble. And who is this?'

'Comrade Martov, this is Comrade Vuokko of the Finnish lathe operators.'

Elli and Martov exchange handshakes and Martov makes some remarks about lathe operators being younger and comelier these days than in the past. Elli replies that he might also find that they have grown more militantly Bolshevik too in recent years. Martov is pointedly relaxed about the barb. Nobody performs being unruffled quite like Julius Martov.

'Perhaps,' he says with a genial, avuncular smile. 'Perhaps.'

After he has moved on, Elli Vuokko makes the group around her laugh by saying that if she spent too long with comrades like Martov she might revise her ideas about there being no need for a war between men and women.

'I wonder if he's ever been to Finland? He wouldn't last too long back home with those attitudes.'

'Some comely young lathe operator would give him a mouthful he'd never forget?' asks Litvinov.

'Never mind the lathe operators, the bloody *seamstresses* would tear him apart in Tampere. They'd rip him a new arsehole.'

'I like you,' says Litvinov.

'Of course you do. Why wouldn't you?' says Elli, but her eyes flicker over to Koba. It is just the briefest of glances but it is a clear and definite moment. His stomach fizzes.

The air shivers.

After their soup and with a long session in a dark hall ahead of them, Koba and Litvinov take the opportunity to stretch their legs. As they step out of the church and into Hackney's hazy sunshine, treading carefully in order to avoid the turds, they are confronted by two solemn urchins.

'Stan!' said Litvinov. 'Have you come bearing sandwiches?'

The boy looks crestfallen. 'Was I meant to? Would you have bought them if I had?'

Litvinov laughs and ruffles the boy's hair. 'No, my young Comrade, don't worry. In any case now I know what butterine contains I may never eat it again.'

Relieved that his professional reputation as a fixer is intact the boy relaxes, though he also smooths down the hair disturbed by Litvinov's paw; he seems to find untousled hair more becoming in a young entrepreneur. Litvinov lets him continue with his grooming for a moment or two before ruffling his hair again as he asks who Stan's companion is.

'This is Arthur,' Stan says, stepping back and huffily resuming the smoothing of his hair. 'Arthur Bacon. His da has a lodging house in Jubilee Street with a spare room for three people. A big room too. And clean. The house even has a bathroom. A flushing bog an all.'

'A bog?'

'You know, a crapper. A khazi.'

'*Smyvnoy tualet*,' says Koba.

'Yeah, a toilet. You press a handle and water comes into the bowl and washes your business away.' It is clearly something of a miracle as far as Stan is concerned.

'Sounds like a palace. How much is it?'

'A shilling per night. Per person.' Arthur Bacon's voice is tentative with the hint of a lisp on the *sh* sound.

'Expensive,' says Litvinov. He switches to Russian. 'What do you think Koba? A whole shilling? Per person.'

'We should take it.'

'I assume you're getting a commission,' Litvinov says to Stan.

'I get a farthing a day, Arthur gets a farthing a day and Arthur's da gets the rest.'

'Ah,' says Litvinov, 'so the true cost is much less than a shilling.'

'That's how it works,' says Stan. 'We're brokers.' He says the word proudly, stands a little taller, jerks his head away when Litvinov goes to muss his hair for a third time. Successful brokers don't allow that sort of liberty.

'Incredible. You hear that Koba? Even the imps of the street here know how to play the capitalist.'

'It is a nice room,' says Arthur. 'Very airy.'

Arthur Bacon is a beanpole of a boy a couple of years older than Stan, skin the colour of thin milk, melancholy eyes set in a freckled face. Muddy yellow hair cut by a hurried hand and sticking up in jagged spikes. It is like a badly scythed field.

'Only fair that we have a fee,' says Stan. Then he explains that Koba can't really go back to Tower House anyway. 'Gaffer doesn't want you. Nate, the cadger you beat up, he's a steady bed. Pays for a kip all through the summer when most of the other regulars go off for a tramp or to Kent to pick fruit and stuff. Gaffer says you got to look after your best clients.'

'Even if they're thieves?'

The boy says nothing. Rolls his eyes. Everyone's a thief, his silence says. Everyone takes what they can. Whatever they can get away with. Way of the world.

'It really is a nice room,' Arthur Bacon says again. He seems worried that the deal is going to fall through. It seems likely that the men could get a reduction in the broker's fee if they push a bit.

'We'll take it,' says Koba.

'You can take it,' says Litvinov. 'In fact, you have to take it. But it's twice the price of Tower House and that extra sixpence is money I can spend on some little luxuries. Let's not forget that an extra penny gets you a double bed in Tower House and a little cubicle to yourself if you find you need one.'

'We'll get the extra money from the party,'

'Will we though? We are the trouble-making faction and the relevant bean counters are all Mensheviks. No, perhaps you Georgians share the room and leave this big bad Russian bear to take his chances with the rogues of Tower House.'

'I'll persuade the bean counters.'

'If you say so. I'm sure you'll employ your famous Georgian charm to good effect,' and Litvinov laughs and slaps Koba on the shoulder.

Stan and Arthur have witnessed this exchange with concerned faces.

'Ah, sweet little artful dodgers. No need to fret boys,' says Litvinov. 'The deal is on. Koba and his compatriots will take this clean and airy room of Arthur's and I will remain at Tower House.'

He leans down and takes Stan's earlobe between thumb and index finger.

'But you should tell this Nate that if he tries to steal anything from me then I will gut him like a fish. I will stick him like a pig and skin him alive. You tell him that. What will I do?'

Litvinov's jovial tone of earlier has gone to be replaced by a deep and savage drawl, while his accent has thickened. 'What will you tell him? Repeat it back to me.'

'You'll gut him like a fish, stick him like a pig then skin him alive.'

'Good, yes. I'll skin him and make myself a lovely jacket from his worthless hide. I'll gouge out his eyes and piss in the sockets. I have done it to better men than him. Now, scram little fixer. I'll see you later.'

The afternoon dies, slowly, lingeringly, measured out in points of order, angry interventions and questions that are often just excuses for lectures, and not short ones. Again, Koba does not attempt to speak. Occasionally he nods, sometimes he shakes his head, but these occasions are rare. Mostly he sits impassive, unreadable, staring at his steepled fingers.

The delegate from Tampere does speak. She makes a passionate little speech late in the session that livens up the proceedings, if only briefly. A spasm of life before the day fades.

She asks, what are the proletariat's class tasks in the revolution which sharply distinguish it from the other classes in Russian society? This, she says, is the kind of question which the Menshevik comrades are afraid of putting on the agenda of the Congress. They flee from hard facts like shadows from the sun. She tells them the weakness of the Menshevik position comes from the fact that they themselves are split by profound disagreements on these questions. Menshevism is not an integral trend; Menshevism is instead a medley of trends, which are imperceptible during the factional struggle against Bolshevism but which spring to the surface as soon as tactics begin to be discussed from the point of view of principle.

Now a change of gear. She takes a breath and her eyes scan her audience. The voice deepens. She becomes quieter rather than louder as her passion rises. Her audience is pulled towards her. Her face is flushed as she calls for war at any price.

'It is idle,' she says. 'To expect any grants from our

enemies, and the history of the past two years teaches us that such hopes are vain – even criminal – since they necessarily hinder the course of the revolution and delay our ultimate victory.' She speaks of the insult to the memory of those have already died if the party changes course now. She speaks of how the war can yet be won. Of the need for unflinching resolve, of the fact that sacrifice is always – always – a necessary part of any important victory.

'Free nations can only evolve out of streams of blood!'

This is the last thing she says before sitting to excited applause from the Bolsheviks. Some, like Rosa Luxemburg, stand as they clap, while the Mensheviks sit in hard and rigid silence.

Koba applauds her too, but he is restrained, reflective. These are his own thoughts precisely, but to hear them articulated so eloquently by this girl still in her teens is extraordinary. Unnerving.

He tries to imagine his wife Kato expressing herself like this. Tries and fails. Maybe, if she was asked to prepare a statement on her love of Jesus, maybe then she would find some words. Probably not, though. Kato's loves are wordless ones, and her arguments those of the gut not the head. Kato bows to her husband in nearly everything, but on two things she is unshakeable despite anything he might have to say: she believes that a woman's purpose is to care for her children and that anyone who fails to acknowledge Christ as their saviour is going to Hell.

Her worry that Koba might end on a gallows with his soul unsaved is the principal fear of her life, though so certain is she of the Lord's power to rescue even the most lost of his flock that she believes even Koba will be brought back to the Church in the end.

Crazy to compare Kato and Elli. He has chosen Kato

44

precisely because she isn't like the Ellies of this world. Just as he can't imagine Kato at a lathe or leading Red Army soldiers into battle – and it is easy to imagine Elli doing this if the final civil war ever comes about – neither can he picture Elli with a baby, providing docile and unquestioning loyalty to a leader like himself. He can't see her giving the softness a revolutionary commander needs in order to keep himself rested and calm for the struggle.

No, the man an Elli Vuokko needs is a young, handsome, fearless and brainless foot soldier who can be killed gloriously in a noble cause and give her beautiful memories to conjure up on long nights after the final victory is won. Maybe later, when her youthful fire has died down a little, she could have a second husband. A schoolteacher, perhaps, a man who is intelligent, decent and kind, a man with impeccable opinions, but a man who also knows he will always take second place in her heart to the lost love of the war years.

It is in thoughts like these that Koba loses himself as the first sessions of the 5th Congress finally expire.

5

Such Peacocks

The famous Rose Street Club is based in one of the poorest districts of central London, a place full of brothels and often the centre of outbreaks of cholera. In a few narrow streets around here, just yards from the theatres and hotels of the West End, are crammed half a million desperate souls. Originally the home of an education centre for immigrant workers, the club has grown to become a major venue for progressive thinking. Here you can meet radicals of all kinds from all corners of the earth. Revolutionary Socialists from the Russian Empire yes, but also German Anarchists, Irish Nationalists, Indian Nationalists, African Nationalists – Nationalists from everywhere – American suffragists and British free-thinkers of all levels of militancy from hand-wringing non-conformist preachers to actual bomb-throwing republicans.

It isn't only radicals that come here, of course. Artisans who can afford a few spare pennies are attracted by the promise of warm rooms, free newspapers and cheap beer.

In the fug-filled main room a dozen or so Bolshevik men are trying to get two girls, Elli and Nina, drunk. And they are not simply trying to intoxicate with booze either. Flattery is deployed – Elli's speech gets many compliments – as well as an exaggerated courtesy, and unusual attentiveness to female opinion. The men also deploy generosity, happy to spend a hefty proportion of their two shillings a day softening up the women's defences with cheap booze. Elli refuses all offers of alcohol with a smile. Nina on the other hand is happy to say yes. She can match the best of them drink for drink.

There are jokes too of course. Heavy-handed teasing. Innuendo. Banter. The women do much rolling of their eyes, a lot of sly smiling at each other.

'Oh, such peacocks,' says Rosa Luxemburg.

She is sitting on a low stool at a table on the other side of the room, squashed between Koba and Tskhakaya watching this jockeying and jostling around Elli Vuokko and her friend.

'Peacocks?' says Tskhakaya in a tone of surprise for these men are for the most part dressed shabbily and unimpressively in drab suits. But Koba knows what she means. The men are parading the finery of their opinions, displaying the cut of their rhetoric, the skilful embroidery of their historical knowledge, the elegance of their learning, the bright clean expansive colours of their wit.

'She means our brothers are showing off with words,' says Koba. He is too polite to add that Rosa's companion, Leo Jogiches, is one of the peacocks hovering around the young women, half-heartedly wagging the tail feathers of his erudition. Not that he looks like he's enjoying it very much.

'More like jackals at a water hole,' sniffs Tskhakaya. Koba and Rosa exchange a look. They see how their comrade stares at the scene across the room. A gaze of such fierce puritanical scorn that it occurs to Koba that it masks lasciviousness. Is it envy that produces such an intense look? Does the Leopard wish that he was padding around these women, waiting for a chance to pounce? Does he wish that he could parade his own knowledge of revolutionary history, show the sharp claws of his scholarship? Or maybe this leopard is mourning that his muscles, once taut, now simply ache. Is he feeling sorry that's just too old for the kind of foolishness that goes on around the edges of a Congress?

Good to know that the middle-aged philosopher is capable of ordinary everyday vices. It's reassuring.

'I feel I should rescue the poor creatures,' says Rosa. She rises and begins to push her way through the conversations and the smoke.

Those girls don't need rescuing, thinks Koba. Those girls know what they're doing. They know where they are. It's like offering to rescue happy seals from drowning. Or maybe it's really Leo she's rescuing.

Koba notes how pronounced Rosa's limp is becoming. It is worse than his own and yet he feels no kinship, no fellow feeling, no sense that they are similarly damaged and so should stand together against mockery or pity. She annoys him, that's the truth. Her doctorate and her limp are both just ways of getting attention, of getting ahead.

Next to him Tskhakaya sighs.

'Everything all right Comrade?' says Koba

'I was just thinking about how this place kept its name despite no longer being in Rose Street,' and, unprompted, he explains how twelve years ago, in an attempt to shake off a reputation for vice the road was renamed Manette Street, after a character in Charles Dickens' *A Tale of Two Cities*.

'And you will remember that Dr Manette spent many years as a prisoner in the Bastille prior to the revolution so an apt location for Socialists to meet, no?' He pauses and takes a dainty sip at his vodka. 'Thing is, it hasn't really worked. Rose Street by another name does not smell any sweeter.'

It is just possible, thinks Koba, that Mikhail Tskhakaya is

the most boring man alive. And a bad liar, too. He was so obviously thinking about women rather than street names. He should just be honest about it.

'Let's get to our new lodgings,' Koba says. 'And hope that they smell a little sweeter than the last cesspit.'

Followed discreetly by some of the toughest men of the party – can't be too careful around here – Rosa hurries Elli and Nina back to Langton House: she'll get a hansom from there. As they walk Rosa tells them to watch out for left-wing men. They can be as bad as any other men. Worse, because they say all the right things it can be hard to spot the bad ones until it's too late.

The younger women are polite – this is Rosa Luxemburg! – but they don't need any warnings about Socialist men. They know all about them.

'You know what I'd like to do,' says Nina. 'I'd like to fuck a proper English milord. Someone with a castle and hundreds of servants. I'd like to fuck him and then shoot him.'

Elli laughs but Rosa just looks thoughtful. 'I wish someone would fuck Leo and shoot him. Both events might do him some good.'

6

We Should Talk More About This

77 Jubilee Street is in every respect an improvement on Tower House. The room may not be strictly 'airy' or 'spacious' in the manner Arthur Bacon has implied, but it is clean, there is fresh linen on each of the three single beds and yes, there is a flushing toilet. Arthur, more confident now he is in his home rather than out on the street, says that his father often grumbles that it is more trouble than it's worth.

'Da reckons it's all very well flushing turds away but when you're not connected to the main sewers, the septic tank overflows regular and that's horrible. So we only flush it once a day at 10pm unless there's a special need for it.'

'And what constitutes a *special need*?' Shaumian's voice has a bubble of laughter in it.

'Dysentery. Cholera. Some dodgy tripe. Da says if it's proper disgusting, you can pull the handle. Otherwise, I will do it at ten. It's my last job of the night.'

'An important responsibility for one so young.'

The other immediately noticeable thing about the Jubilee Street house is that it is filled with birdsong. A bullfinch in a cage in the kitchen is warbling its heart out, the same tune over and over. A pity that it's such a dreary one.

'This is Edward,' says Arthur. 'He's singing "God Save The King". I taught him that.'

'An interesting choice,' says Tskhakaya.

'I did it to please my da, to make him smile.'

'Did it work?' says Koba.

'Not really.'

'We'll have to teach him something else while we're here,' says Shaumian.

'I've tried but he keeps coming back to the national anthem. He likes it.'

'We can be very persuasive.'

'He's outside in the yard most of the time anyway. Da doesn't like him in the kitchen too much. Don't worry, he won't disturb you.'

As they settle in, Shaumian and Tskhakaya wonder where Arthur's father is and discuss the way that the English seem content to let their children do the work. Everywhere you go in this country it is children you see working in shops and in the factories, children pushing handcarts in the street or selling vegetables in the markets. The people of England seem to rely on their children the way other countries rely on serfs or slaves.

Koba says nothing. Shaumian and Tskhakaya are bourgeois, brought up in houses where children were encouraged to read and think and dream. Outside of featherbedded nests like theirs, the entire world rests on the labour of children. They are the largest exploited class of all, without even the option of riot or revolution, without the benefit of organisation, kept in check by brutality that begins at home.

Koba doesn't just remember his father's efforts to make a shoemaker of him while he was barely old enough to walk, he can still feel it. In his muscles, on his skin. In his guts, in a sickness he has to fight to keep down.

51

But what is the point in explaining? Tskhakaya and Shaumian are good Socialists. They understand about oppression, they can articulate the need for a change in the world order, but they can't imagine how it feels to receive a boot in the face or a strap across the back from those who are meant to love and protect you. From those who, despite everything, you still love.

Their fathers never appeared drunk at their school gates, never took their child's books and threw them in a hedge before taking that bewildered kid across the country and putting him to work in a Tiflis factory before he was ten years old. Their fathers didn't take the meagre wages earned from this work to spend on booze. Their fathers didn't, when drunk on this booze, beat them half to death for saying that they were hungry or for asking for a book to read.

Koba could tell them the stories from this time in his life, just as he could explain the statistics about child labour across the supposedly civilised world. They would murmur and nod and say, of course, and yes we should always keep these facts in our hearts and thank you Comrade for reminding us of our duties here. We must try harder. But they wouldn't feel it. How could they? In fact, they would just resent him for having grown up poor, for being genuinely proletarian. Described in detail, Koba's hardships are a rebuke to them. He makes them feel guilty and no one ever quite forgives those who make them feel guilty.

'I'm going out,' Koba says.

No one asks where he's going. Taking long walks by himself is a thing Koba is known for. He is, as Shaumian likes to say, a creature who needs to pace out his territory, a wolf needing to piss on all the furthest corners of his kingdom and leave his scent to scare off rivals.

Less than an hour later, Koba's wandering has taken him all the way to a fussy drawing room in Grays Inn Road, a room paid for by wealthy supporters of the party. Prints of melancholy ladies, some of them clutching small, anxious-looking dogs, hang in gilt frames on the turquoise walls. There's a deep pile Afghan rug with geometric patterns in sunset colours. An ornate fireplace, complete with gleaming brass coal bucket, tongs and poker. An ivory statuette of a ballet dancer on the mantelpiece. A substantial mirror that makes a large room seem even larger. Decanters of spirits on a heavy sideboard.

Sitting among this opulence are two men who, taken on their appearance alone, could be from a music-hall double act, so different in looks are they. One is small, bald, in his mid-thirties, sitting precise and upright, almost lost in a stiff-backed armchair upholstered in leather of rich burgundy. His companion meanwhile is a thin, rangy fellow, all legs and arms, sprawled across a green velvet couch. His most distinctive feature is an explosion of thick dark hair that springs from his head in all directions.

Newspapers and journals in a variety of languages are scattered untidily on the floor around them. The revolutionaries have made this bourgeois room thoroughly their own, given it the look of a reading room in a Socialist subscription library. Vladimir Illyich Ulyanov – Lenin, the delegate from Upper Kama – and Lev Davidovich Bronstein, currently known to his colleagues as Yanovsky, but soon to become Trotsky. The first is the theorist of class struggle, architect of the militant policies of the Bolsheviks, and editor of the newspaper *New Life*. The other acts as the main link between the Bolsheviks and Mensheviks, and is the one most capable of maintaining the uneasy alliance between these fractious wings of the party.

They greet Koba with warmth. There is wine. Jokey apologies are made that the best they have is feeble French stuff rather than the punchy, full-bodied Georgian varieties he is used to. Koba says that it is all right, in uncivilised places like London they just have to make the best of what is available. The atmosphere is convivial, though an astute observer might be forgiven for thinking the jollity is a little forced, the wisecracks a touch laboured. There is a tension here that is almost, but not quite, masked by good cheer. The air is heavy somehow.

Before they get down to party business, Comrade Ulyanov wants to talk first about an item he has read in one of the French papers. There has, it seems, been a new kind of bank robbery, one where an automobile was used by the robbers to make their escape from Les Flics. A gang had hit the Société Générale Bank in Paris, shooting dead a cashier in the process before fleeing in a limousine. The excited journalist from *Le Figaro* had dubbed the robbers Les Bandits en Auto. He had written that it was his firm belief that this was the very first robbery of this kind, but now other desperadoes will surely follow in Les Bandits' tyre tracks and adopt this same method. It is the dawn of a terrible new age in violent crime.

'An audacious piece of theatre,' says Koba

'I thought as a student of the art of the expropriation you'd appreciate the drama of it,' says Ulyanov. 'Not to mention the technological innovation.'

'Absolutely,' says Koba. 'Though of course it is not the first such robbery.'

'No?'

'No. You find the real industrial advances happen in America these days and so it is with heist-science too. In August last year two men hired a car and robbed the Valley

Bank in Santa Clara of 7,000 dollars.' He pauses for a moment, strokes his moustache. 'Did Les Bandits escape their pursuers?'

The delegate from Upper Kama turns back to his newspaper. 'I believe not.' There is another pause while he rustles through the pages. 'No, they were captured ten kilometres from the bank on the outskirts of the city. There was a shoot-out.'

'So it was in California. The police there cornered our two brave rascals a few kilometres from the bank where they shot themselves in the head rather than be taken prisoner. Of course they used a Ford Model K which is notoriously prone to overheating. What machine did they use in France?'

Ulyanov's little beard waggles as he squints again at the newspaper. 'Something called a Prosper Lambert.'

'Not a bad choice. Six cylinders. Still, no match for a horse when it comes to a getaway through narrow streets.'

'You know about motorised carriages then?'

'I'm interested in any technological advance that may affect the party. Motor vehicles will definitely be used as weapons of war in the future. We should probably prepare for that.'

There is a brief silence. Koba has surprised them again. He enjoys doing this. He knows so much about obscure subjects almost no one else would even be aware of, but then finds he is sometimes ignorant of things almost everyone else knows about. Sometimes someone trying to understand the extent of his knowledge is frustrated because Koba will feign ignorance of things he does know and pretend knowledge of things he doesn't.

Despite all this, Koba is confident that Ulyanov likes him, that he admires his energy. That he appreciates the way Koba is so obviously a full-time worker for the party, and not only that, he is a man prepared to go further than most people in advancing its cause.

The conversation turns to other matters. There is reminiscence about the early days of the uprisings of 1905, the hopes they had then and the defeats since. The prospect of the Tsar's Prime Minister Stolypin launching a coup against the Duma, expelling the representatives of the Left.

Yanofsky attempts to keep the mood cheerful by regaling them with the story of his escape from Siberian exile, the heart-stopping moments, the chases through the snow, the surprising helpers. Koba and Ulyanov listen politely. It is a tale they have heard before several times and it's a good story, but it is clearly destined to be the highlight of Yanofsky's life. The story that will define him. Sad, really.

Eventually they discuss possible outcomes from this Congress including, inevitably, the fact that the tactic of expropriations – with or without motor vehicles – is likely to be suspended in a doomed quest for some kind of moral high ground amongst the bourgeoisie. The Bolsheviks may have won the arguments in Stockholm, but power has shifted since then. Many good comrades are weary of being on the margins. They crave acceptance and respectability. As a result Martov and his centrist allies seem likely to win over the bulk of the delegates, people who are still sentimental about parliaments, people who believe it is still possible to gain power for the workers by conscientiously using democratic processes. The ballot box rather than the bullet. The begging for donations, rather than the seizing of property by more dynamic means.

They can be as respectable as they like, it won't save any of them from Stolypin's necktie.

'These people think that revolutions can be won by fair

play, by sticking to rules drawn up by your opponents,' says Koba. He goes on to say how it is a shame because he had had a particularly ripe target in mind for the next expropriation and it was more or less planned out, with a talented creative team assembled. Ulyanov looks up, eyes twinkling. He looks suddenly impish, like a man about to give a surprise present to a favourite nephew.

'We should talk more about this,' he says. 'Votes aren't everything. Permission of Congress isn't always the final word on these things.'

He speaks about a fundraising salon Maxim Gorky has arranged, and wonders aloud about who should attend in order to make sure they have the best chance of persuading philanthropists that it is in their interests to fund the Bolsheviks, that they might want to be on the right side of history.

'We'll need the prettiest girls and the wittiest men, don't you agree Koba?' says Yanofsky.

'Yes. We need *charm*,' says Koba. He almost spits the word. The other men laugh.

'Oh come on, Koba,' says Yanofsky. 'I've seen you be charming. A rousing song or two in that excellent voice of yours. A good joke. A risqué story. A rough compliment to a lady. I've seen you do all these things.'

Koba sighs theatrically. 'The lengths we go to for the people. If only they knew the full extent of our sacrifices.'

His companions laugh again.

'You see, you're a funny fellow,' says Yanofsky.

Glasses are refilled. Another bottle is opened. It is decided that a selection sub-committee should be formed consisting of the three of them plus Litvinov, who is a specialist in charm. And maybe there should be a female member of the sub-committee.

'What about Rosa?' says Yanofsky.

'Yes, the ineffable and indomitable Rosa Luxemburg. She knows what men like.'

The men grin at one another, clink glasses. Down them. Refill them.

It seems a good moment to speak about extra money to pay for the Jubilee Street lodgings. Koba lets his eye wander across the fittings and fixtures of this well-appointed space – that rug, that couch, that chair, those sorrowful women on the walls. Ulyanov follows his gaze. There is a pause and then he agrees to lean on the party bookkeepers first thing in the morning. Lean on them hard.

'We need our own Les Bandits to be fighting fit,' he says. 'You deserve to have a decent night's rest.'

Before Koba leaves the apartment, Comrade Ulyanov praises his restraint in the argument over his voting rights. 'A tactical silence can often work very well in a debate. I feel sure that if you had spoken up, we may even have lost the vote to make you and your compatriots observers.'

'Sometimes doing nothing is also doing something. You taught me that.'

Ulyanov grips his arm. 'Correct, my dear Josef. And it is surprising how often doing nothing turns out to be the very best thing to do. So many things resolve themselves if you leave them alone. The unimportant evaporates, leaving only what absolutely needs to be done.'

A brief thoughtful silence. He takes off his glasses, polishes them: 'It is, however, a tactic that cannot always be relied upon.'

Only now does he tell Koba what's most on his mind. Only now does he give him a task that absolutely must be done before the end of the conference.

'I have left this problem alone as long as I dare in the hope that a solution will present itself,' he says. 'But now is a time for action.'

Back through streets softening in rain, eyes seem to peep from every doorway. Several times, Koba is sure he sees a shape he knows too well from his dreams, a figure scuttling at the very corner of his vision, a golem who escapes from view when he turns to confront him. He considers standing still in the rain and shouting for this figment, this *fragment* of a person to show himself. If he has things to say, he should have the balls to say them to his face. But the thought of bringing attention to himself from the groups of these other shadows, these disconsolate Londoners who trudge the streets without apparent or direction, keeps him silent.

There is a need for light. Koba stops at a public house called The Water Rat. A fitting name for the clientele here, who have the look of damp and half-starved rodents. He has to wait to get served. The pub is not busy but the barman is one of those who like to make it clear that customers are an inconvenience. Foreign ones doubly so.

Koba doesn't make a fuss. He is patient and eventually he is sitting with a half pint of something dark and unpleasantly cloudy in front of him. Koba isn't even sure what he's ordered. He has chosen his drink by pointing at a random handle behind the bar. Some kind of beer. It doesn't matter much. He doesn't intend to drink it. He isn't thirsty. The price of the drink is just the necessary rent for a stool and space at a table to finish his letter. *Dearest Kato, I am sheltering from the weather in a 'pub'. I am having a real English experience. I am every inch the tourist . . .*

He finishes it quickly, carefully setting the address down

on the envelope in English, Russian and Georgian. He stares at the envelope for a while. If you had asked Koba what he was thinking at that moment, and if he had bothered to reply, he would not have said his wife Kato, whose name was down there on the envelope. Neither would he have said his young son Yakov, or even that he was mulling over the events of the day or possible approaches to tomorrow's debates. Still less, would he have said that he was thinking about the revolution. Not even about the task that his leader has just given him. Instead, if he had decided to be honest, he would have said he was just thinking about the actual shape of the letters crammed on to the small rectangle in front of him.

Three languages are needed to get this letter to Kato. Three different alphabets: Latin to get it out of England, Cyrillic to get it to Russia and the Georgian to ensure it reaches its intended recipient.

If the loops of Latin sentences are like the footprints of domestic pets, the patterns left by obedient dogs in snow, say, something too common to be noticed any more, then the blocky shapes of Cyrillic remind him of the slow steps of working animals. The trudge of oxen. The reluctant stumbling of donkeys. Georgian script by contrast soars rather than plods. Murmurations swooping, looping and pirouetting across the blank sky of the envelope. Georgian is indisputably the most magical of alphabets – that is a simple fact – and yet it is the tool of so few people. No other country in the world uses it.

This is the way of the world. The best things, the most beautiful things, are pushed to one side and ignored, their rightful place taken by those who are simply more strident. Those who dare to take up more than their allotted space. Those who refuse to stay where they belong.

The lodging house is quiet when Koba returns, only a fidgety Arthur in the kitchen reading a magazine. Even Edward no longer trills patriotically in his cage. Arthur is absent-mindedly eating sweets from a bag. The boy jumps up as Koba enters. He seems oddly relieved to see him, tells Koba his compatriots are in bed, probably asleep already. They had seemed very tired.

He offers tea. This really is a nervous child. Even at home he lacks the self-assurance of his friend Stan. Koba waves a hand in refusal. He sits down on a rickety wooden chair and gestures for Arthur to sit also.

They sit in silence for a while, a silence that grows until it fills every corner of the room with a thrum of its own. It is a silence that makes Arthur visibly more twitchy with every moment it lasts.

'Would you like a toffee, Mr Ivanovich?' the boy says eventually, when he can bear the electricity of this quiet no longer.

Koba gives this offer serious thought. 'Yes,' he says, in the end.

Arthur passes the bag. The sweet is good.

'One day,' says Koba, 'one day you must have Churchkhela. This is good but Churchkhela better.'

He is suddenly homesick at the thought of the traditional candy of his home country. Almonds, walnuts, hazelnuts and raisins threaded onto a string with chocolate, dipped in thickened grape juice and dried in the shape of a candle. His eyes mist over. It's funny how nostalgia catches you at moments of rest. Unmoors you. Unmans you.

'Nuts,' he begins. He has an urge to explain the manufacture of this king of all treats to this nervy boy. He stops. He doesn't have the English to describe it to Arthur.

61

Nevertheless, something must have communicated itself to the boy, who nods sympathetically.

'Churchkhela,' he says.

Koba smiles at the boy's pronunciation. 'You must say it fast. And use the whole mouth. *Churchkhela.*'

A thought occurs to him. 'Hey boy. Have you seen Georgian writing?' He shows him the envelope containing the letter to Kato. 'See English there. Russian there. Georgian there.'

'Blimey. It is like snakes,' says Arthur. 'How can anyone read that?'

Not birds then, snakes. Koba laughs. Maybe the kid is right. Maybe the words in Georgian are like snakes coiling and sliding over a pale steppe. Beautiful just the same.

Arthur looks at him now, sees avuncular approval in Koba's eyes, smiles, offers him another toffee. Koba sits and studies him as Arthur tries to return to his magazine. After a few moments Koba leans over and picks it up.

'Hey,' says Arthur, but not fiercely. 'Hey, I was reading that.'

Koba flicks through the pages. The magazine is called *Vanguard* and is full of stories of boys at English public schools. Children of lords playing sports. Cricket. Tennis. Various kinds of football. Stories of war and adventure. Soldiers confronting spear-carrying natives in the jungles of Africa. Cowboys shooting redskins, cabin boys defeating pirates. Ghosts. Spies.

'You like this?' says Koba.

'What?'

Koba tries again, biting out the words this time. 'You. Like?'

'Yes, I like. Why shouldn't I like?' Arthur is making a stab at belligerence. It is not a natural talent of his. Koba smiles. He turns to the cover.

'Two. Duh.'

'That's the price. And not two der. It's Tuppence. Two pence. It's just written two dee, you don't say it like that. Don't ask me why.'

'And these—' Koba wiggles his fingers at the bag of toffees. 'If a man needs some of these?'

The boy looks suddenly crafty, the same look worn by market traders the world over. Somehow Arthur has caught the scent that business negotiations might be opening.

'The same. Tuppence a bag.'

Koba smiles; it is clear that whatever tuppence is, the true cost is probably half that. The boy is looking to take another hefty broker's fee.

'Really?'

'Yes. What are you trying to say?' The shrill whistle that enters his voice simply proves again that aggression really isn't Arthur's forte, though he tries. Koba admires him for that.

'Get me some.'

'All right, but I'll need the cutter up front.'

The boy smiles at Koba's ignorance.

'Money,' he says

'Upfront?'

'In advance. Ma Brown don't do credit.'

'Ma Brown is a wise lady. Here,' He hands over a half-crown; the boy's eyes widen. Koba has done it again – it's obviously too much. 'Any *cutter* left, you can keep. I don't really do change. Perhaps buy another . . .' He gestures at the comic.

'Cor. Thank you Mr Ivanovich.'

The trader in the boy is gone in an instant. The child is back. Arthur smiles now, showing all his bright, white teeth. An unexpected radiance.

This is a child who rarely encounters kind words. Koba feels his heart crack a little.

A noise at the front door, some struggle pushing it open. The rhythm of a drunken man stumbling in. Same the world over, unmistakeable, the two steps forward, one step back lurch of the drunk. The ridiculous waltz of the inebriate. The laboured breathing, the pause as whoever it is leans against the walls for a rest, like a boxer on the ropes, a man attempting to gather his forces for an assault on the next few steps down the hallway.

One glance at Arthur's face is enough to tell you who this man is. If there is one thing Koba knows about it is when a boy is terrified of his father. He reaches out, puts his hand on Arthur's arm. He sees it all: the lacerating words that slash the air around the boy, the curses hurled like sharp stones, the daily humiliations, the sudden eruptions of rage. The boy thrown against walls, his cheek slapped, the cruel taunts about his weakness, his gentleness. The way the boy has cried every day of his life and tried to hide it. The way he would deny it now if you were to say this to him. The fact that, despite everything, he loves his father.

'Don't be afraid,' Koba says. 'Safe here now with me.'

7

Girl Nihilists

Five days into the Congress, Dr Rosa Luxemburg and the Finnish activist Elli Vuokko have achieved friendship. At something like a conference relationships develop fast, after all. Normal processes of getting to know people are accelerated. Rosa and Elli often sit with each other during the debates and after the sessions they spend time together walking arm-in-arm through Hackney streets. They make a cheerful, charismatic couple – they laugh easily and conspiratorially together – and are sought out by the Bolshevik men, including Koba, Litvinov, Shaumian and Tskhakaya who accompany them to public houses. They tease Plekhanov – who is visibly annoyed by it – and Martov, who is also annoyed, though not visibly. His smile never wavers.

Every time the women meet they greet each other by repeating that pain is only weakness leaving the body. It's become their personal catchphrase, a secret signal between the two of them. It makes them laugh every time.

Right now something else is making them laugh. Elli Vuokko has achieved a measure of renown and not just within the party. Today for example the English papers report her speech from the first day. The headline in the *Daily Mirror* is GIRL NIHILISTS and Rosa is having some fun by translating the speech into Russian and reading it loudly with as much pomposity as she can muster. She is aiming for the effect of one of the more self-important members of the Duma and doing a decent job. Mimicry is a useful skill for the professional public speaker, handy in the lecture hall and on the soapbox.

'Listen to this,' she clears her throat. '"The good people of Kingsland, NE, are very nervous about the delegates to the Russian Labour Congress who meet every day in the Brotherhood Church Hall, Southgate Road, watched by many police and detectives. One good lady whose house backs on to the yard behind the mission hall assured the *Daily Mirror* yesterday that she has been unable to sleep since Sunday."' Now Rosa switches into an exaggerated version of that stock creature of comedy, the Russian grandmother, the country peasant, full of fear and prejudice.

'"Them foreigners comes out into the yard and gabbles away something dreadful. They aren't here for no good I'm sure and I don't like it."' She resumes the portentous voice she has allotted to the reporter. '"From this lady's house the *Daily Mirror* saw the distressing spectacle and witnessed the gabbling. It was all very un-English certainly – a crowd of Russians, Poles, Latvians, Finns and Jews smoking and talking excitedly in Russian . . ."' She breaks off for a moment. 'Well, it's quite clear that the nervous lady – if she exists – didn't talk anything like that. I think this journalist dreams of becoming a popular novelist but he reports your speech accurately at least. "This firebrand spoke of bombs and barricades in the same manner that the average English girl will speak of bridge and lawn tennis." Then there are some lines about your appearance which he seems taken with. A delicate bloom of passion on fine features, that sort of thing.'

'Do average English girls speak much about bridge and lawn tennis?'

'I think the reporter doesn't know many average English girls. The point is that you're almost famous, dear and you know what that means.'

'No, what?'

'It means you need to be very careful,' Rosa's voice is sombre now. 'Our fragile leaders get upset when the women get noticed. It's a scientific law. Attention for women causes dyspepsia in men. They don't like it and they start finding ways to put us back in our place. Believe me I know what I'm talking about. I've been where you are.'

'Oh, it'll be forgotten in a day or so.'

'I don't think so,' Rosa sighs. 'But hey, listen to this: "A vote is to be held on the expediency of immediate measures of force. The result is a foregone conclusion. Then will follow the discussion of details,"' she breaks off. 'Well, the result *is* a foregone conclusion but not in the way this reporter thinks. It's interesting isn't it?'

'What is?'

'That there were no journalists in the hall, no detectives either – the reporter has that wrong too. Yet he is able to describe you perfectly while also getting the way the argument is going so wrong.'

They walk in silence, Rosa clearly finding something of significance in the article which is eluding Elli. Eventually Rosa says, 'I wonder in whose interest it is to suggest the party is renewing its commitment to armed struggle when the truth is the opposite?'

But Elli has had enough of talk about the Congress. The sun is shining, there is a fresh breeze on her face and she is far from home walking with her new friend through the streets of one of the great cities of the world.

'Is there anything else of interest in the paper?' she says.

Rosa looks hard at Elli. 'Not really. The death of a famous

racehorse. A Suffragette disturbance at a Liberal Party meeting. A boom in the sales of straw hats.'

'Why is there a boom in the sale of straw hats?'

'Going to be a long, hot summer apparently.'

8

Silently Hostile

Occasionally Rosa is late to the restaurant or the cafe – she has high level discussions with Ulyanov, Yanofsky and Gorky and other senior leaders – and Elli finds herself alone with the men, who are mostly charming, in a heavy-handed kind of way. Some make efforts at gallantry and their skills at this vary. Litvinov is pretty good, though she doesn't trust him. He looks like a love 'em and leave 'em sort. Shaumian is alright, though not as funny as he thinks he is. Tskhakaya is especially bad at it, having the diffident resentful manner of one who fears he suffers from bad breath that his friends won't tell him about. The worst thing about being stuck with Tskhakaya is how his attempts at conversation quickly become monologues. So many facts, so few of them interesting. She hopes he doesn't notice her eyes glazing over. She wouldn't want to be unkind.

Often, Leo Jogiches is there too. Smiling and jovial when Rosa is absent. Frowning and watchful when she's present. All his muscles tensed. His jaw clenched.

The only one of the men who doesn't try to engage with her at all is Koba and, though Elli has to admit that she is drawn to him, his silence makes her uneasy. Occasionally she is briefly alone with him and still he says nothing, which means she chatters too much and, she fears, inanely. She is always relieved when Rosa or one of the other men join them at their table, even if that man is Tskhakaya, though Koba often takes this as his cue to disappear on a solitary evening's hike through the London streets.

Once or twice he even begins his walk before anyone else arrives. Elli and Koba will be talking, he'll finish a sentence and then, with a curt nod, he'll turn on his heel, leaving her standing on her own on the pavement prey to the whistles and catcalls of English urchins.

Rosa says this is unforgiveable bad manners, and also proof that Koba has a passion for her.

Elli laughs at this. 'Yes, he ignores me, is silently hostile towards me, always finds an excuse to leave whenever we're alone and that means he is infatuated with me?'

'Yes, of course it means that,' says Rosa. 'The thing is, you frighten him. Or, rather, you make him scared of himself. He worries he might feel something.'

Rosa seems very certain that she's right about this – 'This is an area where I have expertise' – so the next time Elli is alone with Koba and he grunts that he has to leave, that he has an errand, she finds herself asking if she can go along with him. There's an excruciating moment where she feels certain he will refuse, where she mentally rehearses an unconcerned shrug, but in the end he inclines his head and sighs and she decides to treat this as an emphatic yes.

9

Space for Innocence

If Elli is surprised when after ten minutes they are joined on their walk by a skinny youth with hair like dirty straw, then she is too polite to show it.

'Hello,' she says in English. 'Who are you?'

'I'm Arthur, miss.' And he says it as if he is surprised that she doesn't already know.

'Arthur Bacon meet Elli Vuokko,' says Koba. In Russian he explains that the child is the son of his landlord. 'The man is a pig while his boy is too sensitive for this world. I find him jobs to do for me and pay him for them. He swindles me and is delighted with his cleverness.'

Over the last few days Koba has been spending a lot of time with Arthur. He sends him out for confectionery – mints, sticky buns, toffees – and they sit together and eat them in comfortable silence while Edward twitters his hymn to the royal family from his cage.

On the fourth occasion, Arthur had told Koba that he had something to confess. He had been overcharging him for the sweets. He was sorry, but his father often forgot to give him the money to pay the grocers and the cash he'd conned from Koba helped pay off a little of the arrears. Koba just waved his hand. He didn't care, felt good to be able to help the lad.

'Oi, what are you saying?' The boy's face is crumpled

71

with anxiety. His mouth a thin line, his shoulders tight under his stained jacket.

'I am telling Miss Vuokko about what a good man of business you are.'

'Yeah, sure you are,' but he looks pleased.

'Don't worry,' says Elli to Koba.

'What? Why should I worry?'

Elli laughs. Koba looks suddenly like a nervous child. Like Arthur actually, the same anxiety flashing onto his face.

'You don't have to worry that I will reveal your soft heart to our comrades. Your secret is safe with me.' She turns to Arthur. 'And do you happen to know where we're going? Our friend here hasn't told me.'

'Friend of my da's has a shop in Spitalfields. He's asked me to take him to see how we make shoes here in England.'

'I am a shoemaker,' says Koba, in Russian. 'Or I was, when I was Arthur's age.'

They walk, Elli's attempts at cheerful conversation stumbling into a series of bald questions as she looks around her. Questions like: why are so many people here asleep? Every doorway is filled with horizontal human shapes, some half-covered by old coats or burlap sacks, some with no coverings at all. The inert figures seem mostly male, but there are plenty of women. Children too.

'They've been carrying the banner,' says Arthur.

Elli frowns at Koba.

'He means they've been up all night walking,' says Koba, in Russian. 'A man without shelter is not allowed to sleep in the open at night in London. It's a crime punishable by fines or prison. The principal task of the police here seems to be rousing the exhausted homeless and moving them on, keeping them upright.'

'You'd think these people might prefer prison.'

'Some do. But then again, prison is no picnic.' He explains the prison regimen of back-breaking and deliberately pointless work and its innumerable calculated humiliations. There are fines, too. A man imprisoned for vagrancy comes out in debt, and when he can't pay there'll be more prison, more fines, more debt and so it goes on.

'But it's not just cruel, it's stupid. Exhausted people can't work.'

Koba shrugs. Of course it's stupid. Governments are stupid. Yes, of course these wretches will simply grow more used up and they'll get sick and eventually they'll starve, or they'll be so weakened something else will get them before malnutrition does. Or desperation will drive them to commit the sort of crime that sees them deprived of their liberty for years. All of this is so obvious, it's not even worth talking about.'

'Is there really nowhere for people without shelter to go to at night?' The question is in English and directed at Arthur.

'Of course!' he sounds offended. 'There's the spikes and the Sally Army will let you have a doss if you get to their gaffes early enough and you don't mind a bit of alleluia with your skilly.'

Elli's English is not too bad – Finnish education, even for girls, is justly famous – but none of this makes sense to her.

'Spikes?'

'Casual wards. In a workhouse. You got no scratch for a bed, you can go there and they give you a bath and grub and a kip and next day you spend a morning working for them – maybe unpicking rope or breaking rocks or something and then they let you go in the afternoon and you try to find some work, or get some money somehow and go and find another spike cause you can't come back to the same one two days in a row. Sally Army is the Salvation Army. The God squad. Like a church you can sleep in. The grub is better but you got to sing hymns for your supper there.' He pauses thoughtfully. 'I reckon I'd rather take the spike. Or prison. Or the street.'

They walk on in silence for a bit, Koba keeping his eyes straight ahead, Elli looking hard at the life that surrounds her. The under-sized, misshapen people, the tired and skinny livestock. The children still, dead-eyed and sullen, or, alternatively, running and pushing and shrieking like supercharged geese through the crowds. She's been in London nearly a week but she's been so focused on the arguments in the hall or the discussions afterwards that she wonders if she's even once looked properly at anything around her.

Now she pays particular attention to the faces and demeanour of the women in the streets, especially those of about her own age. They are mostly thinner than she feels herself to be, and she hopes that she doesn't look as tired as they do. They are so wan, so many with a curious bluey-yellow patina to the skin, so many with a haunted look. So many muttering to themselves. So many coughing.

'What is the matter with the women?' she says in Russian to Koba.

'Work. Children. Degradation. All three.' He tells her that if Tskhakaya were here he'd be able to give exact statistics about how long the women work, how hard their labour is and how pitiful their reward. The illnesses their industry gives them. The poisoning from the chemicals used in so many trades that makes them anaemic, that destroys their teeth and bones, that taints their skin, that drives them mad.

He talks of how many of these young women are already mothers of children they can't feed or clothe, mothers of children they have to see waste away in front of them, little bodies laid out in the front rooms of the houses, until their parents have begged or borrowed the money to pay for a burial. And how many of those dead children were the result of incest.

'No innocence within the walls of these houses,' he says. 'You need space for innocence.'

He tells her that in these houses where every room is home to at least one family, the girls are corrupted early and as they grow they suffer everything the men do but have it worse because oppressions visited on the men are passed on to the women. 'If a man is bullied and brutalised and humiliated at work, he will try to expunge the pain of that by doing the same to his wife and children at home.'

He tells her that many of these women don't work in factories or sweatshops but are forced to take their chances on the street selling themselves for the price of a drink or a loaf of bread.

'Prostitution brings industrial injuries too of course.'

She knows all this, but hearing Koba tell it in his flat, dispassionate, slow Russian while at the same time seeing the physical evidence all around her in the ruined faces of her English peers, well, it hits hard, strikes her right in the heart.

She feels a hand search for hers. Arthur. He hasn't understood the words, but he has grasped the feelings those words provoked.

'Do you have brothers and sisters, Arthur?' she asks.

'I used to,' he says. He counts them off on his fingers. 'Danny, Eliza, Jane and Lucy. Danny died when I was three – he was two years older than me. Eliza died when I was eight, she was three years younger. Jane died when I was nine, she was four years older than me. And Lucy, we don't know where Lucy is. She left home about two years ago and we haven't heard from her. Da says he thinks she ran off with a soldier. She'd be nineteen now. Da says we have to treat her as though she's dead too.'

'And how did your mother die?' Elli can't help herself.

The boy shrugs. 'No one knows. One day she went to bed and didn't get up. Stopped eating, then she stopped speaking and a few weeks later she was dead. That was just after Jane died.'

Grief, thinks Elli. Grief is what killed the boy's mother. It's obvious. Grief is another disease that will cause a woman to waste away, an infection as dangerous in its way as anything else in this world.

The boy lets go of her hand.

'Here we are,' he says.

Eight rooms in the house. Seven of them home to more than twenty people – adults and children – and the eighth, right at the top and reeking of glue and sweat, is an improvised shoe factory where five men stoop over lasts attached to a long table heaped with a pile of leather and cardboard. The room is not large, no more than ten feet by seven, and every corner is filled with a pile of finished shoes and boots. Many of them adorned with bows, frills and tassels, a daintiness that belies the circumstances of their construction.

As Koba, Elli and Arthur enter, two of the men turn around and give them a cursory glance for a moment, before turning back to their work.

'How do, Arthur?' says one of the men who hasn't turned around. Clearly one of those men who has learned to distinguish the identities of a visitor by their distinctive tread, or by the way they breathe. A useful accomplishment for the worker who can't afford to take a break. 'How's your da?'

'The same as ever,' says Arthur.

'As bad as that?' says the man. 'Oh dear.' And he breaks into a wheezing laugh that soon becomes a wheezing cough.

'Consumption,' whispers Arthur. 'Early stages though.'

'You a doctor now, Arthur?' says the man. Elli sees the boy blush to the roots of his hair. 'Nothing wrong with my hearing lad.' The shoemaker sounds resigned rather than angry, and he doesn't pause in his work. 'What you doing here anyway?'

Arthur pulls Koba towards the men.

'This is Mr Ivanovich. He used to be a shoemaker. In Russia.'

'In Georgia,' says Koba.

'Come to see how to do it properly have you?' says one of the men. 'Look and learn, mate. Look and learn.'

Elli turns to look through the grimy window and sees the one-storey sheds that cover the back yards of this terrace of narrow houses, makeshift homes for those for whom a room in a house – even one as filthy and decrepit as this – is an impossible dream. From here she can smell cheap fat from their improvised stoves, a smell so strong she can almost taste it.

'Look at Missy there. Wrinkling her nose. What's the matter, doll? We not refined enough for you?' One of the men has paused in his work and is leering nastily, a threatening edge to his voice. 'Don't like to get too close to the animals in their cages, do we?'

Elli turns to look at the man, takes in his starved face, the blackened teeth, the blinking rat-like eyes. There's the rigidity of incipient mania about him. The man that knows Arthur sighs.

'We don't have time for this,' he says.

It is Koba who breaks the tension.

'I would like to buy the lady some boots.' He has to say it slowly and three times before the English shoemakers understand him.

A booth in the Blue Boar public house. Hard wooden benches, gargoyles in the corners where the walls meet the high ceiling. Exposed beams. The whole effect meant to resemble a country church enlivened with cheerful prints on the wall. Scenes of medieval English country life. Happy peasants gathering hay. Merry children dance around a maypole on some village green. Beautiful maidens paddle in a pond at sunset.

Elli looks around at the clientele. No happy peasants. Some loud ones. Some laughing ones even, but despite this you wouldn't call them happy. No merry children. Instead there are anxious girls and sly boys, both sexes with eyes that have seen too much pain already. No beautiful maidens either. Instead there are faces reddened with alcohol and work, flushed with the too bright fierceness of people determined to forget reality. Drink, the age-old solace of the poor and, she thinks, another tool of control. A simple, convenient weapon of the ruling class and one that they can sell to the working poor to use against themselves. There's a kind of genius to it. A cruel beauty in the whole system.

If Man is born free but everywhere is in chains, as Rousseau said, some of those chains are bought by the workers and they place them around their own necks. In Finland the regional government has twice tried to pass laws banning alcohol but the Tsar insists on the liquor trade continuing. Of course he does, it's entirely in the interests of the ruling class. When the revolution triumphs in Finland we'll finally put a stop to it, first thing we'll do she thinks. Save the workers from temptation. Save them from themselves.

Next to Elli, Koba is slowly turning over the boots he purchased for her, examining them closely in a way he hadn't when they'd been in the room where they were made. She half-listens as he tuts at the poor cut, the poor stitching, the poor glue, the gaudy design and as he marvels at the fact that he paid more than ten times what he would have paid for far better boots in Georgia. Still, he brought a few moments of pleasure to the sweated souls in that factory.

'This is the richest city in the world,' Elli says her voice soft. 'And yet—'

She gestures at the throng in the pub, but she doesn't just mean to take in the drinkers here. She's also thinking about the desperate men sweating over their machines, the families in their squalid lairs and dens, the makeshift huts constructed in the backyards of the slum streets. 'These people. All so sad.'

She feels Koba stiffen. 'It'll be sadder still when we have to kill them.'

'What?'

'In the coming wars against Capital who do you think will be in the armies of the financiers and the industrialists? It'll be these people. We'll have to kill or subdue them all. And every dead soldier will leave behind women and children to beg, to sell themselves or to starve.'

She wants to argue with him, to say that the point of revolutionary parties like the one they belong to, of conferences like the one they're taking part in, is to persuade people the world over to join together to use their strength of numbers to take power, but she's too tired to fight.

'No free nations without a stream of blood,' Koba says, and laughs. 'No free Russia, no free Finland and no free England either. No free anywhere without a lot of blood.'

'You think I can't do it? Kill people I mean.'

'Oh, I'm sure you can. Anyone can learn to kill. It's learning to live with having killed that is the difficult part. The living come and go, but the dead never leave you. Everyone you kill hangs around, plucking at your sleeve, wanting to be acknowledged, refusing to be forgotten.'

She wants to know how he can be so certain of this. How many has he killed? Or is it just a form of bragging, like when Jens in the Tampere factory tells her he can tame wolves, that he does it every winter, that he'll show her how one day.

She looks at Koba closely now. His eyes are distant, unfocused. For the first time she thinks he looks really beautiful. Despite the damaged skin, the unkempt beard, the way he hunches defensively in his worn jacket, his profile is noble and there is a beguiling sadness in those eyes fringed by long, almost girlish lashes.

Koba turns and looks at her and smiles, that astonishing, unexpected happy grin. She feels her heart jump in her chest. He grows solemn again.

'The first person I killed was a child,' he says. 'The second was my father.'

Then he stops. Arthur is back with them, somehow carrying three pewter mugs in his slim hands. The boy is all apologies.

'Sorry it took me so long. I had trouble getting served. But here you are.' He hands them their drinks. 'Porter for Mr Ivanovich, draught stout for me and milk for Miss Vuokko.'

'Thank you,' says Elli. She notices that the milk is watery and thin. Serve that in Tampere and you'd be in trouble.

'Is it all right?' asks Arthur, anxiously. Koba is right, the boy is so sensitive.

'Yes, of course,' she says.

'Good work,' says Koba. 'Any change?'

'I thought you didn't do change,' says the boy but he begins to fumble in his trouser pockets.

'Keep it,' says Koba, and he smiles. 'You're right. I don't do change.'

10

All We Have

'And so what happened?'

'What happened when?'

'When you went on your walk with Koba.'

It is the end of another day of futile wrangling and Elli Vuokko and Rosa Luxemburg are in the German cafe that Rosa particularly likes. Round tables, sturdy chairs, clean napkins, sunlight streaming in through big windows, good strong coffee, even proper pfannkuchen. It's not like Berlin, obviously, but they could be in Danzig or Leipzig or somewhere.

'Nothing happened. Really nothing. We walked but we didn't talk much. Sometimes he pointed out a piece of architecture he found unusual. Occasionally he looked in a shop window. We had a drink. We looked at London and its sorry people. We went back to the house where he's staying.'

'Oh, yes?' A raised eyebrow, an arch smile, a flicker of pink tongue.

'And nothing. For our whole walk we were chaperoned by a sad-looking boy who lives in in Koba's lodgings, who made us a cup of tea and showed us his little bird, which he has trained to sing the king's national song.'

Rosa sits back with a sigh. Her chair creaks. 'The English are so peculiar.'

'Then he escorted me to Langton House, where he shook

my hand and thanked me for being such a pleasant companion. He didn't seem like he was being sarcastic though I feel sure he was.'

'He's definitely got a passion for you.'

'Yes, I agree, the evidence is absolutely overwhelming.'

They order cakes.

They've been here a few times now, munching ginger-bread while discussing the need to take on the real enemies of the revolution, by which they mean the safety-first Mensheviks. The men who are, in the end, more dangerous to the fate of the working classes than the Tsar. The men they will have to take on and defeat and soon. Martov, Plekhanov and others will destroy all they have worked for if they let them.

This is already an old topic. The starting point where they begin before moving on to other things: the vivid energy of the London streets, the beauty of the Finnish countryside (Rosa Luxemburg had spent some of last year in Kokkola); the inevitability of prison.

Rosa welcomes the idea of prison. Time to rest and think, to concentrate properly on her writing. 'What a haven it is,' she says.

She tells Elli – who has always been frightened of prison – that as a political prisoner in Germany they let you write letters, they bring you clothes and books. They cook you three simple meals a day.

'It's like being a nun,' she says. 'Like being on retreat. Of course, I miss male company. But not that much.'

Elli says nothing. She likes Rosa, admires her, finds her fascinating and wise. But can she really be so relaxed about being locked away by the state, about being at their mercy? Anyway, Elli suspects that what she says is only true for bourgeois educated women. Factory women might have it harder. People she knows who have gone to prison, well, they've gone and come back broken. Sometimes they haven't come back at all. They've died of mysterious diseases, even when they were in perfect health before their arrest. Or they have been killed 'trying to escape'. Or they've just disappeared.

Maybe Rosa doesn't mean what she says. One thing Elli has learned about Rosa is that she prefers a bold statement to a truthful one. And if they start bickering about this kind of comment she might not get to hear about Rosa's love life and that would be a shame because it is compelling, wonderfully dramatic.

Elli has enjoyed hearing the story of her friend's romance with Leo Jogiches and grown sad at her descriptions of the way it has unravelled, the light of it dimming into weary grey routine, until Rosa had found another love, a passion that gave her new life but has also invigorated Leo, only not in a good way.

'I had a letter from Kostya today,' Rosa says now.

'Exciting,' says Elli.

'It would have been only it was brought to me in bed. By Leo. Brought to me opened and read.'

'He's intercepting your mail?'

'I should have anticipated he would.'

As she leans forward in her low basket-work chair that groans like a rusty gate when she moves, as she drains her cup of the last of the dark bitter coffee that Rosa prizes so much, a thought occurs to Elli. Maybe Rosa *had* anticipated that Leo would read the letters from her lover. Maybe she had wanted him to. Maybe this is one of those complicated games that long-term couples play.

Rosa's lover is Kostya Zetkin, the twenty-three-year-old son of her old friend Clara Zetkin.

Elli has seen a photograph. Rosa laughed when she produced it. 'He is not a beautiful man. I mean, handsome enough but a bit heavy around the jowls maybe. He will have to guard against becoming plump as he gets older, but what he does have is a beautiful mind. Scientific, clear, direct. He writes that way too. And he's passionate about life, about changing the world.'

'And about you.'

Rosa had smiled, a little sadly, Elli had thought.

'Yes, about me. I think I'm terribly bad for him actually. Or rather I'm probably good for him now but I think I may become bad for him later.'

'Now is all we have.'

'No,' Rosa had replied. 'We never have now. Tomorrow is all we have. Or the idea of tomorrow. We always seem to live in the future not in the present. Then we get old and find that actually the past is all we have, the place where we live. We move from dreams to memories in the space of a heartbeat.'

After a pause she says, 'It's very hard for women to avoid becoming mothers to their men anyway and when you are thirteen years older, well . . .'

'Tell me what happened when Leo brought the letter.'

Now Rosa brightens as she describes Leo's rage on reading the latest example of the clear, scientific prose of his rival. Her voice quickens and her gestures become larger as she talks about the way he had shouted. The way he shook his clenched fist in her face. The way he threatened to kill her. The way she laughed at first and then became really scared.

'I'm only nineteen and I know you don't laugh at men,' Elli says.

'Yes, it's something girls have to learn early. Men can't take being laughed at, but I've known Leo so long I've forgotten some of the basics. Forgotten that he is a man. He did calm down in the end, but I had to lie to him. Had to assure him I would never leave him.'

'But you will leave him.'

'My dear, I have already left him. I left him years ago.' She smiles at Elli's puzzled look. 'Listen, even when we are in the same room, even when we're in the same bed, I am somewhere else. If he accepted that then he would be happier too. I don't know why some people persist in clinging to what makes them miserable. It's as if the ship they are sailing on has sunk but instead of holding on to the wreckage that floats they make a grab at what is bound to drag them to the ocean floor. It's a shame because I really did love him once, really felt we could make proper human beings out of each other, and if he let me go I would still feel affection for him. We could still be friends, could still help each other, be good for each other, but now . . . I don't know.'

'You feel you might end up hating him?'

'Worse than that. I'm going to end up pitying him.'

Rosa takes out a cigarette, and lights it in a graceful, practised manner, inhales deeply, but then makes a face. Exhales and coughs. 'That's the last time I buy these. They're the new hygienic ones, I got them from a charming little shop near the Houses of Parliament, a place where they do some interesting blends. These are meant to be healthier than other kinds. Meant to be good for the lungs. They certainly taste nasty enough to be medicinal.'

She gives Elli a cool, apprising look. 'You're very good, you know.'

'Why? What am I good at?'

'You don't know? I can't believe others haven't told you. You're the perfect audience. You listen so well. You're never completely silent, always encouraging me to say a little more on any subject whether that is the economics of the German state or what poor old Leo is like in bed. It's true that I never need very much encouragement, but still you're good at getting the meatiest gossip. You'd make a good secret agent actually.'

'What?'

'Certainly you'd make a better spy than the ones I usually meet.'

'You meet spies?'

'Of course. Every night.'

'Where? Why?'

'The why is because I can't avoid them and the where is at the hotel. The Three Nuns is full of sinister characters. Ladies who gentlemen sit down with but don't remove their hats for, if you know what I mean. Lowlifes with desperate, red-rimmed eyes. Crooks. All of them wanting something very badly. Drink. Money. Love or the approximation of it. Addicts of one kind or another. The definite spies are a Dr Bunin and his wife and their craving is for information. They are not very good at their job though. Too obviously prying into my business. They don't quietly encourage revelations the way you do.'

There is a long pause. Rosa Luxemburg lets this silence continue until the point where it feels uncomfortable. She takes a draw on her cigarette. Coughs again.

'These really are vile. Another thing girls should learn: what brings you pleasure can't be good for you and vice versa.' She laughs. 'Dear Elli, your face! Don't worry. I do not think you are a spy. Though the party is riddled with them, and it's certainly true that some of our most active members will be working for our enemies. After all you wouldn't invest in those who are useless would you? You'd want the best people.'

Which is when she tells Elli that she had been suspected of being a police spy once.

'1896. Here in London. I was twenty-seven. First time at a Congress as a fully recognised delegate. I spoke against Polish independence and the leader of the Polish delegation said I'd been sent by the Tsar to bewitch the Polish men, to make them doubt themselves. That was Ignazy Daszyński. I'm Polish but because I didn't agree with him on the future of Poland, I had to be a traitor. I was a good-looking young woman. I stood up to him and that was also treachery. Honestly, Elli I sometimes think men are too emotional and too lacking in intellectual rigour to be trusted with leadership.'

Elli looks at her steadily. Even jokes about such things are dangerous. Careless talk can cost you – and your friends – everything. Elli is sure Rosa knows this. Is sure she is testing her somehow.

'Nothing happened to you?'

'Of course not. Daszyński is an idiot. He just can't argue, can't think on his feet, and that was obvious to everyone,' Rosa frowns. 'My God girl, your eyes.'

'What about my eyes?'

'They're like fire. I'd like to draw your face one day.' She stabs the cigarette into the ash-tray with a sudden decisive gesture. 'I feel I've spoiled the mood, ignore me. I'll get the bill.'

Once outside in the breeze, they can both relax again. A lady on a bicycle passes them, her bell tinkling indignantly.

'I know I'm meant to approve of ladies on velocipedes, but I find I can't. I think they're just too ridiculous.'

Elli can't agree. She recites the reasons bicycles are an unequivocal good. Cheap, fast transport for the workers travelling to factory or office, Let's not forget that travel time is always unpaid. For a few pounds the worker on his Raleigh is suddenly the equal of a rich man in his carriage. More importantly he is a match for the policeman and soldier on his horse.

For women, the bicycle is even more important. The chance to move fast, unencumbered and unchaperoned, through the streets, to leave the city, to get good healthy exercise, to escape pursuing men if they have to.

'Unless the men have these machines too,' Rosa says. 'And the men will get the best machines. The fastest ones. A bicycle might just become another weapon in the war on women. Something else for our sisters to be afraid of.'

Rosa steps delicately over a pile of horse-shit. Elli admires her black button boots. They're not new but they are good quality, built to last. Unlike her own. This is the first time she's worn the ones Koba bought for her and it will probably be the last. She can feel the blisters growing with every step.

'Oh, I know you're right,' Rosa goes on. 'After the revolution we will probably give bicycles to every worker. Just seems that what benefits the workers as a class, doesn't always benefit women as a class. Or not as much as it should. Anyway, I just wish that for once the future would arrive and not look even uglier than the present.'

'I like your boots,' says Elli.

'Well, we must try and find some similar for you,' says Rosa smiling. 'Lots of good German boot-makers in London.'

Later, in her clean, pale room in Langton House with the sound of a girl singing a hymn softly somewhere nearby, Elli will wonder why she hadn't told her friend the whole truth about her walk with Koba. The look in his eyes when he told her he'd killed a child. The way he had smiled straight after. Weakness had left him and taken everything important with it, leaving a hard shell behind. They hadn't mentioned it again on the way back to Jubilee Street, nor when they'd left there for Charlotte Street. No, they'd talked of much else – the mountains of Georgia, the fields of Finland, being the only children left alive in a family – but not that. It was just as well, because what would she have said? Nothing that would make Koba feel anything, she is pretty sure of that.

11

Emily Fucking Bronte

Rosa and Elli skip weapons training and instead wander the second-hand bookshops of the East End, chatting inconsequentially about the birth of the new Spanish prince and why the English papers seem to think this worthy of so many columns of gushing prose, when they are approached by a small man, apple-faced behind his wispy beard. A man with blazing eyes, a man fizzing and popping with anger.

'English!' he shouts. 'When in England speak bloody English! Language of bloody fucking Shakespeare!'

'I beg your pardon, Sir,' says Rosa brightly, her accent barely noticeable, her speech accompanied with her most charming smile. 'You should calm down. You'll give yourself an aneurysm. Perhaps take a seat and get your breath. Count to ten.'

The man leans into Rosa's face, whiskers quivering with outrage, 'Bitches,' he hisses. 'Bloody fucking bitches. Shakespeare! Charles fucking Dickens!'

'Don't forget Emily fucking Bronte. George fucking Eliot. Elizabeth fucking Gaskell.' Rosa says, still smiling, her voice still warm, still pleasant.

The man looks confused. 'Bitches,' he says again. 'Foreign bitches.'

With that he lurches away, loose-legged and unsteady. Stumbling straight into the puddles and the turds.

'Drunk or a lunatic?' says Rosa. 'Could so easily be either in this country.'

'Could be he's both.'

'True.'

'I've noticed that the people here get strangely upset by hearing other languages. I wonder why that is?' says Elli.

'It makes them feel stupid,' says Rosa. 'How can you believe you're the master race when everybody else speaks more languages than you do, when they even speak your own language better than you do? And these people around us,' she waves her arm vaguely. 'They're self-obsessed enough to think that we're speaking about them. That we are making fun of them or keeping secrets from them. A very paranoid race, the English. Worse than Russians even. If only they knew how little we care about them, how little thought we give them.'

They walk in silence for a while. Then they walk with Rosa talking one minute of hats and the next of guns. She is fascinating on both subjects. Elli could listen to her talk about anything for hours. Which is just as well.

Rosa is not entirely unaware of how much she controls the conversation, however. 'Next time my dear, we will talk about you. I insist.'

'There's not much to tell.'

'I'm sure that's not true. Not with those eyes and that face. There must be men.'

'Trust me Rosa, there are many subjects more interesting to talk about than me and men. In any case why should we talk about romance at all? I'm sure the men aren't gossiping about love.' She stops. She has the idea that she has been too vehement, too aggressive.

Rosa does not appear offended or even taken aback. She just laughs and links her arm through Elli's.

'I can assure you that the men are much bigger gossips than we are. They are obsessed by romance. Though of course they hate themselves for it. Next time we are alone, I will tell you why a dalliance with Koba before you leave London will be good for you both. God, I wish I was nineteen again, instead of an old lady of thirty-six.'

When they part Rosa embraces her, kisses Elli on the cheek. Her body is warm and she smells of coffee and fruit. She holds her for a long second.

'Pain is only weakness leaving the body,' she breathes.

She kisses her again.

12

Something Inside His Heart

The Duke of Wellington is one of those quiet narrow bars you find in the side streets of the West End of London. The kind you think will be crowded but never are. Tired men, sitting alone, minds empty, staring into space, lingering over their pints of porter, avoiding going home. It is not one of the pubs the revolutionists ever use.

Dr Bunin and his pretend wife had buttonholed Koba in the street while he was on one of his walks. Had plucked at his sleeve on the Tottenham Court Road at about eight in the evening, and suggested, courteously enough, that he might like to go to a public house, to join them for a small libation. Koba had replied, in an equally courteous tone, that they might like to go and fuck themselves right in the arse. Yet here he is, sitting quietly while the smirking doctor with the whistling voice enumerates all the ways in which the Bolsheviks are getting hammered in the Congress.

'Defeat on every front. Losers on the battlefield, losers in the streets, losers in the Duma, losers in the conference hall. Your forces in retreat everywhere. Thoroughly outman-oeuvred. If some future scholar ever writes the history of the party the only giant emerging from the pages will be Julius Martov. Martov. Imagine that.'

The man giggles like a girl, already tipsy on half a glass of filthy English beer. Unless he has been drinking earlier, which is possible. The Okhrana are not all that fussy about who they employ. It seems rogues of all kinds can find a job with the Tsar's secret police and that includes drunks.

Dr Bunin is enjoying himself. He grows loquacious: 'Armed struggle is a dirty phrase now, isn't it? It's all constructive engagement and compromise and building coalitions. It looks like the bank raids will be forbidden soon. Instead you're going to raise money with charity bazaars, tombola booths and bingo. Oh, and yes, you won't be above begging off friendly capitalists, of course. No such thing as dirty money now. You'll take anybody's. Congratulations, Josef, you finally have a party that's in your own image.'

Bunin apparently finds this all highly amusing. A huge joke. His companion, on the other hand, seems to find his manner contemptible. Her body language, distant and distracted when Koba had first met her, today suggests that she finds Bunin tiresomely vulgar. He is an embarrassment to her.

Perhaps they are married after all.

She doesn't even seem to be listening to her partner, instead staring about her, finding the few other occupants of the saloon of much more interest than either of the men sitting with her. Koba watches her carefully as Bunin talks. He admires her long throat, her haughty features, her skin the colour of dark sand. The way she draws on a cigarillo held between gloved fingers. He wonders idly if she's Jewish, before returning his attention to the buzzing-insect voice of Bunin.

Keeping his own voice carefully neutral Koba says that, it's true that right now things are not going so well for his faction. So what? No one ever said that creating and sustaining a revolution would be easy.

'Of course not everything is going badly for Comrade Jughashvili,' says Madame Bunin. She sips her thin pale wine. Funny how in England the unspoken rules around who drinks what are the exact reverse of those in Georgia. Back home the ladies drink red, the men drink white. Koba has a sudden yearning for the golden qvevri wine of his home district.

When Dr Bunin speaks again there is a sly, dirty undertow to his voice. 'Indeed not. I believe the subtle pursuit of a certain Finnish factory worker is going very well. That's a campaign which looks like it might end in triumph. Some skirmishes have already been fought successfully. Many coffee breaks are taken with Miss Vuokko. And there has been at least one lovely walk with her around Whitechapel and Hackney. I believe they got as far as Spitalfields. The whole walk taken up with lengthy discussions of policy objectives no doubt. She's even been to his lodgings in Jubilee Street.'

Koba closes his eyes. Allows himself the luxury of imagining an axe smashing into this man's face. Once, twice.

'Well, I suppose a man might get lonely when separated from his wife and infant child. A man might then throw himself into his work,' Bunin says.

Koba doesn't reply at once. He's still imagining the destruction of Bunin. His head turned to pulp. Brains and blood on the table, on the carpet. The pub silenced. This condescending bitch forced to look at him properly. Forced to take notice of him. He sees himself rise from his stool, wipe the handle of the weapon carefully with a cloth, lay it on the table and walk slowly through the pasty-faced, slow-thinking English workers with their slack jaws, and their empty eyes. The screaming would start just as he exited the place.

He takes a breath to let the vision evaporate. Sighs and

leans across the table. Puts his hand on Bunin's arm. Looks him right in the eyes for stretched seconds. Notices the yellowy tinge to the whites of them. Yes, Bunin – if that's his name – is a weak man. An habitual sot no doubt with the sad grey pallor of the compulsive onanist.

He keeps his voice low. 'Why are we here? You know what they'll do to me if our connection is discovered?'

'I can guess.'

Koba runs through some possibilities anyway. His body might turn up in a random alley, probably bearing marks of torture. Maybe his body parts will turn up in several places. Maybe they'll find the torso in one town and his head in another, genitals sliced off and placed in his mouth. He speaks about some of the more inventive deaths that have been meted out to informers over the years. The slow slicing technique with the condemned tied to a post while skin and limbs are gradually removed. The scaphist killings where the informer is covered in honey and tied up in some deserted place known for its vermin and left there to be gradually nibbled to death over a few days. Or maybe the end will come with a hungry rat placed in a upturned bucket on the stomach, this bucket heated from the outside so that the desperate rat tries to escape by burrowing downwards, chewing through any flesh and organs in its way.

As he goes over these imagined fates, he keeps his eye on the lady. He is hoping that she'll shift uncomfortably in her seat, that her mouth will purse and he'll see a flush spread over her features, but she seems unruffled. Bored, even.

'I've read the reports,' she says. 'You were turned very easily. A few roubles. Prospect of avoiding a modest prison sentence. That's all it took. A threat, a small bribe and you were ours.'

The implication is clear: his death by rat will be entirely

appropriate as far as she is concerned. He looks at her steadily. She doesn't turn his way, continues to look at the drinkers around them, drawing hard on her cigarillo as if she is on a stage. She is both detached from her surroundings yet at home somehow.

It sets off something inside his heart. He remembers how in his first weeks in the shoe factory at Tiflis a butterfly, wings a spring morning blue, came in sometimes, rested on a workbench for a few minutes, before it rose languidly into the rafters high above the noise and sweat. A pulse of unconcerned beauty that carried its own world with it wherever it went. Madame Bunin is a creature of that type.

Dr Bunin takes another sip of cloudy beer and speaks again, quite cheerfully. 'In any case the point is moot. We won't be spotted by any of your comrades, and if we are, well, you'll have a story. I have faith in you. Perhaps you should have a little more in yourself. You're a resourceful man, Mr Ivanovich. Quick-thinking. Famous for it. Here's an explanation you can have for free – my wife and I were lost in these teeming streets and you helped us with clear and precise directions and now we are repaying you with a drink. We are Russians, every little service is repaid with an offer of a drink. And you are Georgian. Georgians never refuse such an offer. Even from Russians. In any case, my dear Ivanovich, we had to make contact somehow. Every night we have been waiting in Kettner's and every night you have failed to appear. And it's not as though we get a good meal to compensate. Kettner's is not great you know. I don't know why the *Pall Mall Gazette* recommends it. The food is bland and overpriced, and the service is poor unless you get one of the German waiters. The Germans are not too bad.' He sits back, thumbs in the pockets of his waistcoat, so pleased with himself. Then decides he has more to say.

'I'll be candid. We are under pressure to justify our salaries. This business we're in, it might be new, but it operates much like any other. We have superiors and they also have superiors. You're a salesman in the field and we're the people in the office and our job is to make sure you're working to your full capacity. What you have to remember is that above us there's a head office and everyone there needs to look good to please the owners and the shareholders. We're all judged on results and you just haven't produced any recently. That looks bad for all of us.'

Bunin goes on to remind him that just before Koba had made the trip to London, the Okhrana had given him a total of 1,500 francs of hard currency – foreign exchange that the service couldn't really spare – just to ensure that Koba could come and report on the Congress for them.

'And yet you are unable to advance our interests because you don't have voting rights and haven't even given us any information. You should know that we have other sources of intelligence.'

He lets that implication sink in. Perhaps the Okhrana don't need Koba. Perhaps he is surplus to requirements. If they ever need to trim their workforce, perhaps Koba will be one of the ones they let go.

The lady speaks. 'It's time for diligent employees to prove their usefulness. Others are doing so.'

'Fuck you,' says Koba.

'Oh, very witty Mr Ivanovich. You're full of bon mots today.'

Koba sighs and makes a decision. He tells these two about the wretched task that Ulyanov has given him.

'You've been entrusted with rooting out informers yourself?' Madame Bunin is smiling as she says this, her face transformed, almost radiant. It's almost worth sitting here in this humiliating interview in this grubby bar, just to see it. Almost, but not quite.

'Yes, Ulyanov has become convinced that we have another Azef situation.'

'An Azef situation. That's very serious.'

Yevno Azef, the former head of the party's combat organisation, was the man who had organised the assassinations of both the Minister of the Interior and the Governor of Moscow. Azef, it turned out, had been working for the Okhrana for over ten years ever since he was at university and offering to inform on fellow students for cash.

The success of these two killings had given Azef huge power within the party. Because he had proved himself – because he was a hero – he was able to gather evidence against many senior party activists and give up their names to the Okhrana. This list included Anna Yakimova, a veteran of the conspiracy to kill Tsar Alexander II, and Zinaida Kopolyannikova, who had been hanged in August last year for the assassination of the Colonel of the Tsar's lifeguards. In total, thanks to Azef, seventeen senior revolutionary leaders were arrested before he was himself betrayed by an Okhrana officer who had become a convert to Marxism.

It had taken that officer nearly a year to persuade anyone of Azef's guilt. No one wanted to believe it. A Court of Honour had sat for a month trying to weigh the evidence and by the time it was concluded, Azef had disappeared. The party still had agents across Europe looking for him. The problem was that after Azef's success, people of talent were now scarce in the organisation. The hunted was a first-rate mind being tracked by the mediocre.

'Whoever it is, Ulyanov wants him – or her – unmasked by the end of the conference.'

'Unmasking, meaning...?'

'Dealt with, yes. Properly.'

'Ironic.' Dr Bunin chuckles and burps. He is not transformed. It is not worth being anywhere to see this man laugh. He slurps at his drink. Some misses his mouth, drips on his jacket and his shirt front. 'Whoops.' He giggles.

'All very difficult,' says his colleague. She is still smiling, showing all her teeth, but it is not a smile that reaches her eyes. 'What will you do?'

Koba shrugs. 'Perhaps I'll just convince him that he's paranoid. I'll say I have conducted a full investigation and that there is no traitor. That there could only ever be one Azef.'

'Will he believe that?'

'Maybe. Or perhaps I'll tell him that he overestimated my detective abilities and that there is a traitor but that I have been unable to discover their identity.'

'He'll be disappointed in you. Might retard your progress in the party.'

'I'll have to risk that.'

Koba closes his eyes again. Breathes in deeply. The quiet despair of the thoughts of other drinkers seems to fill the place like poison gas.

'There is another possibility.' Mrs Bunin is contemplative now, serious. And he's ahead of her. Knows where's she's going.

'Yes, I know. I could throw him a bone. A juicy one.'

'You could, but who?'

Who indeed? Who will constitute a juicy enough bone? Who can they sacrifice? Someone high up enough to make it worthwhile, but someone without serious defenders in the party. Someone Ulyanov already suspects or dislikes or fears is getting too popular. Someone who is inconveniently blocking Okhrana penetration into the upper echelons of the party. Koba has already gone over this in his head many times and he has the beginnings of an answer.

'It should be a centrist. Someone who is making the party too respectable. A leading Menshevik. After all, it's in your interest that the party remains a threat to peace. Who would fund an operation to oppose a beast that is already tame? Who pays a matador to fight a bull that no longer gets angry, that no longer has the stomach for a fight?'

'Yes, of course it's very important for us that your party stays aggressive.'

This is the paradox all intelligence operations contend with: to be successful is to ensure their own abolition.

'So. Martov, then,' Koba says. He just wants this meeting to be over now. He is tired and he has the beginnings of a headache.

'It's a thought. But maybe he is just too juicy a bone. Too unbelievable. We'll discuss it with our superiors. You're right though, this might be a real opportunity for us.'

The insufferable doctor opens his mouth again. At least the smirk has gone. 'You don't think you're compromised? That he suspects you?'

'He might. Ulyanov suspects everyone at least some of the time. And some people he suspects all of the time. I don't think I'm one of those, but it is possible. I mean, if Azef was a spy then how can you trust anyone?' A pause, then he finds that what is in his heart spills over. 'You know, this might be a good time for me to be getting out.'

Dr Bunin lights a cigarette, takes a delicate sip at his drink, winces, but at least the beer finds its way to his mouth this time.

'Is that how you think this works then, Mr Ivanovich? One last success and then retirement with a generous

Okhrana pension? A new name in a new town. A disappearance to some far-flung part of the empire. A quiet pen-
pushing civil service job. Something in the ministry of
culture maybe? Something not taxing anyway. I know, you
can write reviews of all the latest seditious literature for us.
And you're still young. Not even thirty. You have time to
build a career. You might, in time, become an Executive
Officer. Imagine that! A quiet, tidy, easy bourgeois life. A
decent house, dacha in the country, good school for Yakov
and any other children that come along. Some nice clothes
for Kato. A maid maybe. Yes, that would all be very lovely.
Perhaps you could even return to writing your little poems.
"But I shall undo my vest! And thrust out my chest to the
moon!" That's one of yours I believe.'

Koba looks hard at the man's sloppily cut, over-ambitious
hair, his badly tailored suit, his sarcastically smiling face,
the way he is leaning over the table with his greying beard
too near the glasses. Again, he entertains the fantasy of an
axe demolishing the man's smug features.

'Only that's not really a feasible career trajectory for you
is it?' says Bunin

No, Koba has to stay where he is, rising as high as he can,
being as useful to his paymasters as he can for as long as he
can. The alternative is not a quiet job as a happily faceless
bureaucrat, it is that the Okhrana cut their losses and turn
him loose. Everyone knows how that ends – he's just sketched
that out for them himself. A horrible death and his new wife
widowed, his new son fatherless, his reputation destroyed.
Koba the disgraced. Koba the unmentionable.

Madame Bunin sighs. She gives Koba a quick direct look,
blinks hard and turns her head to where the late sun is now
slicing through the window, revealing the dust as it twists
and dances in front of them. The smoke from her cigarillo

floats in an almost perpendicular line upwards. A thin silver strand spiralling towards the high ceiling. Like the tough but delicate thread of a spider's web.

'There's no easy way out of this for you,' she says. 'Best you can do is let us decide who the informer is, then let us make sure there is irrefutable evidence of their treachery, something that corroborates your accusation and we'll work together on how to best present this evidence to Comrade Ulyanov.'

'We will be condemning an innocent man to death, of course.'

'Or woman. And, please, it's too late to get squeamish now. In any case none of you are innocent. Especially not Martov and his kind. Not that I'm saying we'll choose him. But don't worry, you'll be rewarded.' Her voice is rich with contempt.

Her husband chimes in, 'Anyway, Mr Ivanovich, *Koba*. We had always assumed working for the Tsar in the way you do is not so much a job as a calling. A real vocation. I mean you do it so well. Carry out your duties with such vigour.'

Koba ignores him, keeps his eyes on the woman. Her long neck, her fine skin.

'Tell me more about the ways I might be rewarded. There must be some bonus you're allowed to authorise.'

Mrs Bunin's shoulders twitch and what, he wonders, is that shrug telling him? That he'll get to live a bit longer and in this day and age this is a good reward and he should be grateful? That he might get back to Tiflis and the chance to see his wife and child again? That living is itself the bonus? Or is she just saying that she's bored and wants to head back to her hotel? Maybe she also has a headache coming.

Koba waits a few moments. Takes a long drink of his beer. He needs a minute or two to construct what he wants to say. To make sure he's got it right. The right words in the right order pronounced correctly. This bloody language.

He stands abruptly. Fixes the room with burning eyes. Scratches at his right cheek.

'Stop!' he says in English and loudly enough to cut through the pub's sad murmurs. 'I will not sit here and have this country slandered!'

His voice is strong, rich and deep. Full of controlled passion. There is beauty in it. Now he turns to address the whole room. Waits until he knows most of the drinkers are looking his way. 'This country. It has given me refuge. Shelter! Given me hope! I will not sit with you while you insult it. While you curse England and her king!'

He knows his accent is poor so he makes sure to speak slowly. To bite out every word. He raises his glass, holds it out to the other drinkers, encompasses them all in the wide sweep of his arm.

'To the king! To England! Down with her enemies!'

With that he slings down another swallow of murky ale, pushes his way through the saloon bar and out into the streets.

Perhaps nothing will happen. Most likely thing is that the handful of lonely souls in The Duke of Wellington will barely look up from their drinks. Bloody foreigners, they'll think, bringing their obscure quarrels here.

Yes, it might be like that but he prefers to imagine some London tough, some Empire-loving thug, four or five drinks in, at the stage of drunkenness where he is prepared to take offence at anything, swaying over to the table of the Bunins and demanding to know what they were saying about the king and about their country, insisting that they explain themselves. The hope is that this fat patriot – and he will be fat, Koba is sure of that, these thugs always are – will threaten to avenge the country's insulted monarch. Maybe that same fat patriot will give Bunin a slap, and if he does then that weasel will piss himself for sure. Maybe he'll lay urgent groping hands on the supercilious tits and arse of the phoney doctor's pretend wife. It is a shame that he won't be there in the room to see her lose her composure, to see panic finally flare in her eyes.

He remembers now that the delicate pale-blue butterfly in the factory had been swatted by a foreman who had cursed it and who had shouted over the protests of the other shoemakers that it was a distraction. It had to go. Anyway, he had said, butterflies were the most dishonest of all creatures. They seemed beautiful at first glance but look closer and they had all the ugliness of any other insect. In fact they were more ugly, they were properly monstrous. They gave him the horrors and so he had killed it, and what the fuck anyway, if people didn't like the way he ran things they were free to find another factory that would employ wretches like them. Oh, and by the way, they would be wretches arriving at the doors of those factories without references.

That had been the day Koba had left the place, the day the envoy from the priest came to rescue him, to take him away from the brutal hands of the father back into the hard but protective embrace of the mother. It was a happy day, possibly the happiest he had ever known and yet he had wept for hours over that butterfly and he feels some of the same grief and anger now, though he couldn't have said why.

13

Filth Like This

In Jubilee Street Koba finds Shaumian and Tskhakaya are sitting up with Arthur Bacon. They are talking about life in a future Socialist state, explaining to the boy how different things will be once the workers of the world own the means of production and distribution.

'Everyone gives what they can and takes only what he needs—'

'That means enough food for everyone, a house for everyone—'

'A flushing toilet for everyone. And all of them properly connected to the sewers—'

'Free drinking water—'

'Hot water for washing—'

'Decent clothes—'

'Shoes. Good shoes. Bad shoes will kill you—'

'Doctors for everyone—'

'Dentists—'

'Time for recreation—'

'Time for girls—'

'Paid holidays!'

'School for every child for as long as they can benefit from it—'

'No kings. No princes. No dukes—'

'Everyone gets a say in choosing the leaders—'

'More important. Everyone gets a say in organising their work. The worker is the expert so he should decide how his job is done.'

'No churches. No lies about heaven and hell ...'

'Imagine a London where everyone has enough to eat, and somewhere warm and safe to live. Where the ruling class have been vanquished. Where the police are on the side of the workers.'

'Where there are no police at all!'

'Where no one needs to commit a crime to get the money to eat.'

'Imagine a London that doesn't stink.'

'Sounds nice,' says Arthur, politely. Which makes the men laugh and tousle his hair and pinch his cheeks. Nice!

'In a Communist England they won't be letting you read filth like this,' says Shaumian. He is flicking through *Vanguard*.

Arthur flushes, snatches it back. 'What's wrong with *Vanguard*?'

'Propaganda for the British Empire. All these handsome young men shooting tigers, capturing the dark-skinned villains. Showing them what's what.'

'Just stories,' Arthur shrugs.

'Nothing is just a story,' says Tskhakaya, gravely. 'Every printed word is a brick in the building of a world. Every writer is an architect and the writers of this journal, they have designed a prison for your mind.'

'Leave the boy alone,' Koba growls in Georgian as he plants himself on a kitchen chair. It's not just his head that aches now. All of him feels stiff and bruised. His ankles feel swollen. 'And buy him some more sweets tomorrow.'

Shaumian and Tskhakaya look sheepish. While they have

been talking they have also been munching their way through Arthur's toffees. Ma Brown's paper bag lies almost emptied on the table. They hadn't even been aware they were doing it.

'He needs to stand up for himself,' mutters Tskhakaya.

'The kid is simply paying for his education,' smiles Shaumian. But to Arthur he says. 'You shouldn't let people – even people like us – take your things. We will repay you tomorrow.'

'I don't mind,' says Arthur.

'You should mind,' says Koba.

Koba knows Arthur's whole history. Knows that there had been a steady parade of 'aunts' coming to live in the house to look after him after his mother died, but that they always left, weeping, after a few weeks or months. Arthur was always relieved to see them go because, although their arrival meant days of peace and even laughter, those days were followed by a much longer period of arguments and fights.

Sometimes the police were called. It was all right because the police were often on first name terms with Thomas Bacon and would josh him and tease him and do no more than wag their fingers at him, no matter how grotesque the accusations from the women, no matter how obviously bruised they were. Still, Arthur's fear was that one day his father would go too far and the police would have no choice but to arrest him. Maybe it would be all right now, there hadn't been a new lady, a new aunt, for over a year now.

Arthur loves his father. Will do anything to make him proud. Already he runs almost everything at 77 Jubilee Street. He cooks, cleans, buys the provisions and changes the sheets.

'And you do it well,' Koba had told him. 'We thought

there were spirits doing it. You are so fast and so quiet. You'd make a good thief.'

'I don't do everything,' said Arthur. 'Da makes a damn fine full English breakfast sometimes.'

He told Koba that it had been his father who had brought his bird Edward home late one night, had named him after the King. He told him how his father used to tell him stories when he was young. Stories of pirates and highwaymen. Koba knows how important it is for the boy to believe that his father is fundamentally a good man and his heart cracks a little.

Now Koba finds himself telling this shy, mixed up boy that he hopes his own lad, Yakov, grows up to be as efficient, capable and as kind as Arthur Bacon. Shaumian and Tskhakaya exchange amused glances and Koba is sure he has used the wrong words and if they are the right words then they are probably in the wrong order, but he must get the sense across because the youngster flushes with pleasure. Koba feels another stab in his heart.

Koba vows that one night, he will tell the boy better stories than the ones in *Vanguard*. He will tell him tales about the original Koba, stories of robbery and daring and of defeating monsters in high mountain passes. Maybe he will tell Arthur some of his own stories about shoot-outs with the police in Tiflis and Batsumi.

For now he fishes in his pocket and digs out a half-crown, the head of a choleric old man seeming to stare at the world with reproach. Crowned heads are meant to be uneasy but this man – the head of the greatest Empire the world has ever seen – just seems irritable. It is not the head of a monarch who fears rebellion, but rather the face of an ageing playboy whose bones are beginning to creak. Someone who can no longer contemplate a day without an afternoon nap. Just another middle-aged man approaching redundancy and impotence. A half-crown indeed.

He gives it to the boy. 'For sweets. And maybe we get your da's famous English breakfast tomorrow?'

A shadow passes over Arthurs face. 'I can ask, I suppose.' He scampers out of the house, heading off to pay some small debt of his father's no doubt.

'A lovely gesture,' says Shaumian, smiling. 'You spoil that boy.'

'Yes,' agrees Tskhakaya. 'He doesn't need candy or pocket money or adventure stories. He needs the discipline of a good school. He needs science and learning. You can kill a good brain by too much indulgence as it develops.' He attempts a smile. 'I hope this isn't going to be how you are with Yakov.'

Koba frowns. It seems his fate to be surrounded by fools. What does Shaumian know about what spoils a boy? What does Tskhakaya know about killing anything?

That night the old dream. Shadow and rain. A crowd murmuring in the half-light, smell of horses rising off them. A man half-dragged, half-pushed into the centre of the platform. He should be hooded, but isn't. He looks around wildly, as though searching the crowd for someone, a friend, a saviour. Koba knows his face. Of course he does. In the dream it is always his father's face. The man has his hands tied behind his back. A priest recites from a heavy bible. The hangman waits. The priest finishes his recitation. There is silence. Stillness.

Sudden confusion. The condemned man shouting while policemen grab his legs as they kick. They bind them. A rough sacking hood finally placed over his head. The noose wriggled into place around his neck. His words have become muffled, indecipherable, a blur of agonised noise. He'll be asserting his innocence, or begging forgiveness. He'll be cursing everyone there, calling the crowd ghouls and vampires and the children of whores.

Then it's done. A lever is pulled. The man on the scaffold drops.

Everyone hears the neck snap.

A moan rises from the spectators, the low and hollow susurration of horror that always accompanies this moment, however deserving the criminal.

There he is. Dangling and jerking, that obscene dance on the end of his rope. Koba looks away, at the hot and reddened faces of the crowd, the disgusting way they lick their lips. He looks at the blank indifferent sky, but he is drawn back to the scene on the scaffold after a minute or so. The body is still now, just another carcass, no different from the pigs strung up outside the butchers on Nia Street in Gori. The hangman removes the hood, the moan escapes the crowd again. The hangman looks as if he might bow, the end of another excellent performance.

Koba wakes with a start to hear his own gasping shallow breaths, to feel his heart bouncing in his chest and to hear soft weeping from somewhere in the house. A boy is crying but trying to hide it. Koba tries to ignore it, to concentrate instead on the quiet snores of the others in his room. Shaumian and Tskhakaya sleep peacefully.

What do they dream of?

Soft hands of their lovers. Gardens. Nothing that matters. Nothing that counts.

At breakfast, a doughy, puffy-eyed Thomas Bacon shambles around the kitchen promising the revolutionists a treat of fried eggs and thick rashers with all the trimmings: kidneys, sausages, oyster mushrooms, fat toms and toast. He is another typically small Englishman. Disappointed eyes in a lard-pale face mapped by tiny broken veins. A fussy way about him, a habit of pulling at his collar as if it was too tight then at the waist of his trousers as if fearing they were about to fall down.

As he stumbles about the long table, prodding with a spatula at smoking and spitting frying pans, swigging from a heavy china mug, he mumbles a nonsense song about a bicycle made for two. He is in a good mood.

There is a sweetness on his breath. Koba estimates he is on his second mug of alcohol- laced tea.

This is the best their landlord will feel all day, the head-ache and sickness he always has on waking melting away with the application of whisky and now he feels strong, happy, content. He will feel less so with the next drink and his temper will continue to curdle and sour throughout the day. His irritation will increase, turning eventually and inevitably to anger, and with that will come a desire to punish the world. To vent his frustration, to expiate his pain. He'll want to break things and the thing most likely to be in his way, the easiest thing to break, will be Arthur.

When the food is piled greasily onto the chipped white plates, when the tea is poured and the white bread smeared with butterine, he launches into a complaint, something that has been eating at him.

'Not being funny, lads. But could you do us a favour?'

They wait.

He doesn't look at them. Speaks his next words as if to his own plate. The man is a coward as well as a drunk.

'Could you lay off giving the boy ideas.'

They wait some more.

'I mean could you stop filling his head with nonsense,

about there being a paradise on earth.' He looks at his guests, sighs, gives them a sorrowful bovine stare. 'All this socialist shite.'

Now he gives them his own considered rebuttal of the works of Marx and Engels, the distilled result of a thousand conversations overheard in public bars, in shops, on trams and the omnibus. The half-remembered arguments of newspaper editorials. Comes down to this: Socialism doesn't work. People are naturally competitive. You'll always have inequality. It's just the way of things. Some people are clever, some people aren't. Some people work hard, some people don't. Why should the stupid and the lazy get the same as those with brains? The same as those who sweat and strain to feed their families? Good housing for all. Clean drinking water. Free schools. Free hospitals. These are pipedreams. Might as well wish for unicorns. It's just not possible, not here in England at any rate, and even if it was how would we pay for it? No such thing as a free dinner.

And so on. All the time he's talking, Koba is thinking that there is something wrong here, there's something missing.

The revolutionists listen politely. At least they do until they've finished the breakfast, until they are on the second round of toast and jam. Until Thomas Bacon starts on about the obvious folly in giving the vote to women, in allowing more democracy in the colonies, the disgusting immorality of getting rid of the royal family and the House of Lords. These things are fundamental to the national character. Do all that, he says, and England will hardly be England any more.

'It's bad enough now,' he says. 'I go outside sometimes and it doesn't even feel like my own country. Jews and Hottentots and Hindoos and God knows what everywhere. We've lost control. We need things to go back to more like how they were.'

'Oh,' says Shaumian. He is smiling. 'What time should we go back to, Mr Bacon?'

Bacon doesn't even need to think about this.

'Waterloo. The time when we stood alone against Napoleon. When we saved Europe. We won that war, not that you'd know it now that we're the dumping ground for every scoundrel from all four corners of the globe. Now that cheap goods come in from all over the Empire.'

'You think Britain doesn't benefit from the Empire?'

'It's a millstone round our necks. Nothing but trouble. We brought civilisation and religion to the most benighted places in the world and what do we get? Grief. Nothing but grief. Not a word of bloody thanks. So we might as well clear off and leave them to it. Let them murder each other, and eat each other and whatnot.'

Shaumian laughs, Tskhakaya grunts, frowns, opens his mouth to speak.

'It's not worth arguing,' says Koba, in Georgian. 'Let's just finish our meal and get going.'

'No, I'm enjoying this,' says Shaumian.

'Textbook case of false consciousness,' says Tskhakaya.

'His political position is confused certainly,' says Shaumian.

Thomas Bacon stops, makes a visible effort to control his annoyance at their speaking their own language. Tries hard not to be provoked. Takes a long breath, blows his nose noisily into a handkerchief. Clears his throat. Tells them he is just saying that he doesn't want the boy's head turned by impossible dreams.

'He's soft enough as it is. You'd think not having a mother might have toughened him up, but seems to have made him go the other way. Anyway, decent regular job, nice girl, couple of kids, the chance to save a bit to send them to school, the hope that they'll look after him in his old age, that is the best he can hope for if he works hard, stays healthy and keeps his nose clean. Maybe a couple of jars on a Saturday night. A bit of a sing-song now and again. What you've got to understand is that what you can get away with in the sort of places you come from won't ever work here.'

'Mr Bacon, with all due respect, what do you know of the sort of places we come from?' says Shaumian.

'I read the papers. Anyway, enough said. Hope you don't mind me bringing it up.' A pause, then: 'Did you enjoy your breakfast? A proper full English sets you up nicely for a hard day's plotting.'

'Where is Arthur right now?' This is Koba.

'He's sulking somewhere because I got rid of that pissing bloody bullfinch. Was getting on my wick. Doing my crust in.'

Which is when Koba realises what has been missing. Edward and his mournful chirruping of 'God Save the King'.

Outside the Brotherhood Church, waiting for the women to finish the exercise class, Shaumian and Tskhakaya talk of the stubborn refusal of the English working class to consider alternatives to the brutal system they are living under. Koba doesn't join in. Such a futile discussion. Of course those without the space to dream can't see the value in it. Of course those with almost nothing fear that the little they have will be taken from them, feel that they dare not gamble with it.

A better world depends on an alliance between those who have nothing whatsoever to lose and those who have enough leisure to imagine alternative futures. Those who have time and education enough to read and think. Who have time to stare at walls and daydream. This is surely clear to everyone who thinks about it for even a moment.

While the others chatter, Koba thinks about what his life

116

would have been like if his own mother had died and he had been brought up by his father. A father who believed Koba was the product of adultery, who resented him because he alone had been spared in the smallpox epidemics that killed his siblings.

The beatings would have been worse and more frequent and, God knows, they were harsh enough and came often enough anyway. The time he asked for money to buy paints and his father threw coins at him. He was cut on the cheek but knew that his father had been aiming for his eyes. The time the father threw a hammer at the son for chipping a plate. He had missed the target then too, but not by much.

It was a beating by his father that led to his crippled left arm. Blood poisoning following a fracture had nearly killed him. The only medical treatment offered was an ointment prepared by a peasant whose rudimentary knowledge of herbs was gleaned from his grandmother. That gluey gunk might have helped his recovery, who could say, but Koba believes the chief reason he survived was because he has a special task to undertake. A mission, a destiny important for the progress of humanity.

And that time he was knocked down by a carriage in the streets. His mother had spent all the money they had on calling a proper doctor. His father would not have done that, would not have wasted good *chacha* money on medicine for an idle daydreamer.

His father would not have allowed him to go to school either. Would have insisted on his becoming a shoemaker. And there would have been no one to take him out of the factory once he had started there. Left to his father's care, Koba would have lived a short, brutish life and died young. Young and unmourned. More than that: unnoticed. One more filthy speck on the manure heap of history.

14

Fun

For ten minutes after the morning's self-defence training, Elli and Rosa can't do anything other than slump in stupefied silence on the bench they have just used for step-ups. They are exhausted and in pain. They sit and listen to the savage grumbling of their bodies. Muscles protest, tendons mutter mutinously – even to take a breath prompts ribs to complain in no uncertain terms. They are also sheathed in a slick patina of sweat.

Edith Garrud has really done a number on them. If pain really is just weakness leaving the body then this time it had a party before it went. Really trashed the place.

Eventually, Elli recovers enough to suggest that it's maybe time to get ready for the first meetings of the day, to help set the rows of chairs out. Rosa asks her what's the big rush? Nothing is decided in the mornings.

'I am a woman with a fragile hip. I've just been tortured for an hour. I'm not doing anything until I've had a long hot bath. I'm not spending another day perching on one of those ridiculous chairs itching and sniffing my own sweat!'

Elli laughs. Her friend sounds as if she is rousing tired troops to storm some Bastille.

Rosa smiles. 'Besides,' she says in a softer voice, 'I can do without Leo seething beside me, stopping me thinking by radiating his negative energy.'

She nods to the door of the hall where Leo Jogiches has just entered with a group of other men and it's true that he wears the scowl of a man spoiling for a fight. He glowers at them.

Elli laughs, 'Yes, all right. I agree. It's true. Nothing happens in the mornings except men talking.'

Which is how, ten minutes later, Elli finds herself at the Haggeston Baths around the corner in Whiston Road.

'A cathedral of cleanliness,' says Rosa, and she's not wrong. The Haggeston Baths are new and housed in a sternly impressive building, one that rises above and dominates the rows of small shops on either side. A bright, clean, solid lavender-scented future intimidating the scruffy and dirty past. The baths are busy, too, the noise of laughter and splashing echoing off the tiled walls.

Whoever thinks the poorer classes enjoy the dirt in which they are forced to live has never been to Haggeston Baths on a weekday morning.

It is obvious that Rosa has been here before, that she knows her way around. She pays the entrance fee and hires towels for them both from a bored child at the front desk and leads Elli to the vaulted room at the back of the building. Within minutes they have undressed in the chilly communal changing room, stowed their clothes in lockers and are stretched out in neighbouring slipper baths, washing with fresh soap, Elli's head angled so her plait is safely hanging over the tub's edge away from the water.

Up to now Elli has appreciated the spartan bathrooms and the warmish water you can use to fill the wide sinks in the YWCA, but here in Whiston Road is a whole other level of comfort. The water is so hot, the clouds of steam so thick, she could almost imagine herself back in Finland, back in the saunas of Tampere. She feels a sudden pang of homesickness.

'Beautiful, eh!' calls Rosa through the steam. 'And these are just the second class baths. Imagine how they get to wash in First Class! What do you think the difference is? Beautiful men to wash your back? Others to towel you dry? Still, this is good enough for me for now.'

To Elli's astonishment, Rosa begins to sing. She sings 'The International'. In French, too. She has a good voice, resonant, deep. And loud of course. Loud, clear, tuneful, but still, Elli expects the occupants of other tubs to call for her to shut up and let them bathe in peace. As Rosa moves through the verses, Elli fears they will threaten her with violence if she doesn't stop. It is not, after all, a very cheerful piece.

No one says anything, no one does anything, though Elli fancies she can feel the air vibrate with disapproval. Maybe this is the famous British reserve in action.

If so, it is the second instance of this famous British reserve she has witnessed in the last half hour. The first occurred when they were getting changed. The other women in the room had gone to extreme lengths to avoid catching a glimpse of the bare flesh of their fellow bathers, keeping their eyes fixed firmly on places where bodies weren't. They also undertook some serious contortions to reveal as little of their own skin as possible. Displays of such flexibility that Mrs Garrud might have admired them if they'd taken place in the fitness class.

Rosa, typically, had commented on it. And not quietly.

'They're only breasts. They're only cunts. Everyone here has got them. What is wrong with these women? Why so shy? They're beautiful! All of them! Even their scars are beautiful!'

She had gone on to say that when the day comes that women can look at each other directly, when they can appreciate their shared experience and collective strength then that's the day they will find themselves running the world. Yes, when that day comes they will know the revolution is on the point of succeeding.

'What man could stand against us? What man would even dare to try?'

When she's finished singing Rosa says: 'You know my favourite line in that song? *Nous ne sommes rien, soyons tout!* We are nothing, let's be everything!'

She is in a skittish, giddy mood and her voice is light as she insists on keeping the conversation fixed on Elli. She asks her about working in a factory, is it not miserable and hard? Does she not find it oppressive working with uneducated men all day, however much you feel for their situation?

Elli replies that yes, working in a factory can be miserable and hard, but the other workers, men and women, make it almost worthwhile. They are funny. That's a big thing. A major plus. You can bathe in a constant river of laughter all day long. Has Rosa ever noticed that the more people rise in life, in any field, the less funny they become? The richer you are, the less of a sense of humour you have. The more power you gain, the less you laugh.

Rosa says yes, it's a thing she has noticed too. Powerful people are rarely funny and find it difficult to laugh. Especially at themselves.

There's a silence where Elli closes her eyes and luxuriates in the hot water, feels tight muscles unwind, feels the grumbling of her body quieten. Listens to the cheerful chatter of the women around her. They talk of the sweetness of children, the baffling ways of men, the difficulties of keeping a house clean, the family fed and how hard it is to find even five minutes for themselves. How tired they are. She can't make out exact words or follow whole conversations, but she knows this is what the women are talking about because it is what women always talk about. London. Berlin. Paris. Tampere. Timbuctoo. In the reservations of the American West, most likely. The conversations are the same everywhere because the problems are the same everywhere. She wonders if men knew how good it was in here for women, would they find a way of taking it away from them.

After a few minutes, Rosa breaks in to ask about her childhood so Elli tells her of the best things: the safety of the fields and open spaces around their home. The way the local children could play in the snow unsupervised, unlooked for. And hunting, of course. Those long, long summer days when her father would take his ancient rifle and their dogs and they would trek silently for miles looking for deer.

'You can shoot?'

'Yes, I can shoot. Not as well as my father and I haven't done it for a year or so, but yes I can shoot.'

'Well, that is a good skill to have,' Rosa raises her voice in a good approximation of Mrs Garrud and shouts, in English. 'Every woman should know how to shoot!'

'Too right,' says a cockney voice from one of the other tubs. 'Too bloody right.'

Rosa laughs again and asks Elli what the worst thing about her childhood was.

Elli struggles to answer. She thinks hard. The biting cold sometimes, the difficulties in moving around in winter under so many layers of clothes. The midges, of course. Rosa has been to Kokkola, she knows about the vicious Finnish midges. But, no, now that Elli thinks about it, her childhood was a happy one and she feels suddenly ashamed that she has never thanked her mother and her father for their gentle care, their quiet constant love. She feels unmoored, on the point of tears, but Rosa tunnels into her thoughts again by asking, as she has often threatened to do, about Elli's relationships with men.

'You must have them fighting for you in Tampere?'

'No, no fighting.'

Elli thinks of the men and boys she has had encounters with, a history of shy glances from boys she likes interspersed with all the times – too many times – when men she doesn't care for have grabbed at her at unexpected moments: on the way back from school when she was younger, and on the way back from work now. Hands touching her arse on the tram, lewd propositions from builders and draymen. Commonplace irritations of the sort every woman has to put up with. Not worth speaking about to Rosa.

'You are at an age where you need an intellectual man.' Rosa laughs. 'I mean, handsome enough naturally, but someone older. Someone like Leo in fact.' She laughs again as she takes in Elli's horror-struck face, 'You don't think he's good-looking? He needs someone. Or, rather, I need him to find someone but don't worry, I'm not trying to palm him off on you. You'd probably be too much for him anyway. You might destroy him. He was impressive once, but I'm not sure he can hold his own any more. No, you need someone who will be a guide, but also be prepared to learn from you. Someone with the confidence and experience to become an equal partner. I on the other hand, am of an age where I just need a bright boy, a boy who has just one thing on his mind and can keep going all night.'

'I thought it was the scientific precision of Kostya's thinking that you liked.'

Rosa laughs. 'That too, of course.'

Elli imagines that in later years she will think about this conversation often, about the time she lay in the bath while one of the foremost leaders of the revolution lay next to her giving her romantic advice. She thinks she might have many conversations with friends, party members, children, grand-children that begin with an excited question: you knew Rosa Luxemburg? Wow, what was she like?

To which the future Elli might twinkle and say, well, she was very keen on finding me an inappropriate boyfriend. She sees herself recounting for them verbatim Rosa's next words.

'Married men are best for girls your age. They're not as needy as the bachelors: they can't own you and know that they shouldn't try. And they're often pathetically grateful for any excitement in their lives. Just don't let them leave their wives for you. It can get unnecessarily complicated then. Horribly stressful. Shall we get dressed?'

Rosa stands. Stretches her arms above her head. She's not shy, she takes delight in her body and when Elli stands, she's frank in her admiration of her new friend's body too.

'Yes, so beautiful. Don't let it go to waste.' A pause. 'It would be a shame for the Congress to end and for you to go back to the factory without having some sort of adventure. It would be a waste of the lathe operators' investment in you, don't you think?'

Which is when she tells Elli that she has been selected as part of the Bolshevik delegation to the party being given tomorrow night by the soap magnate Joseph Fels.

'It'll be work – we're after donations obviously – but it could also be fun. Maybe you'll meet a rich, married British man there.'

'Yes, I can imagine exactly how much fun that would be.'

Rosa laughs again. Claps her hands.

'Well, Koba is going too. So you'll have a backup plan.'

Walking back to the Brotherhood Church, they pass Koba standing on his own leaning against a wall, staring into space. Rosa nods, smiles, passes a few pleasant remarks, smiles at his curt responses. Elli loves how her friend is so easily amused, one person with power who still knows how to laugh. Koba doesn't intimidate her with his severe stare and his brusqueness. Better men than him have tried to overpower her in this way. She's immune.

Rosa hugs Elli then walks on.

Elli stays to make conversation, to ask if they missed anything at the morning session. It turns out Rosa Luxemburg is not always correct, and sometimes things do happen in the morning meetings. Sometimes it's not just men performing their silly talk.

'They had the final vote on the expropriations. We lost, by the way.'

Elli feels a sudden queasiness. 'How many votes?'

Koba gives one of his rare smiles. Again, Elli wonders at the magic of it, the way it completely alters the architecture of his face. How it makes him sort of handsome, distracts the eye from the cratered skin. Makes you forget his limp and how short he is.

'Don't worry. We lost by a lot more than two.'

'That's a relief. I suppose.'

They stand in silence. It's not awkward. It's companionable. Elli feels languid. The workout, the bath, the chat about love and sex with Rosa Luxemburg. She feels freer at this moment than she has ever felt.

'Koba,' she says. 'This Congress will be over soon and I'll be going back to Finland and you'll be heading back to

Tiflis and all we've done so far is listen to speeches, to indulge in ineffectual talk in smoky rooms. We have had one long walk together. We bought some useless boots. Anyway, I don't know about you, but I feel the need to have some fun.'

'Fun?' he seems genuinely puzzled by the word.

'Yes, fun. I'd like to play at being a tourist for at least one day before we all go back to our real lives. I'd like to wander around London, see the sights – the real sights – somewhere other than the vile holes the people here are forced to live in. Maybe undertake the adventure of a trip on the underground railway. I don't think anyone will much miss us. You never speak in the debates anyway,' she says.

'But you always do.'

'And everyone ignores what I say. So what about another walk, explore the city properly?'

There's a long moment where he looks at her appraisingly. She finds herself blushing. Has she been clear enough in spelling out what she wants? Too clear perhaps? The moment stretches on. Now they are no longer companionable. Now there is awkwardness.

Koba seems to come to a sudden decision. 'Why not? A walk. An afternoon off. Fun. I can do fun.'

15

Distractions

In her room, Rosa is restless. She tries to write a bit, turning her lectures from the university into the beginnings of a book. *Capitalism is the first form of economy with propagandistic power; it is a form that will extend itself over the globe and eradicate all other forms of economy – it tolerates no other alongside itself . . .*

She stops there. Stands. Stretches. Sits.

It's no good, the words are hiding. They are there, she can sense them, but they won't fully reveal themselves yet and she doesn't have the energy to hunt for them.

Instead she works on a letter to Kostya. She tells him to avoid risks, she tells him how she longs to hike through Switzerland with him. She tries to tell him that she feels like she is hovering over an abyss, but that she's not sure why this time. She tells him of the need for more clarity in her life, to focus ever more narrowly on her work. She tells him about Leo's murderous looks at her during the Congress sessions and how much pain this gives her, though she takes care not to show it, to seem lightly dismissive always. She tells him of her new Finnish friend and her nameless worries for her. Then she asks after Mimi. Is that naughty cat behaving herself? She tells Kostya that it is because of Mimi that she wishes to return to Berlin as soon as possible. Here she pauses and sucks on her pen. It's a joke because of course it's

Kostya she really wants to see most. But then again, is it? Are all relationships with men not just distractions from the central task of a life? Isn't it true that her animals have given her more pleasure?

She writes for a while longer, but her concentration is broken. She knows Kostya wants to read sexual hunger in her letters, he wants written evidence of her desire for him – men can be such policemen about this stuff, such lawyers – but she is not up to that just now.

Eroticism can be harder work than political writing. So often when writing of sex, when trying to properly express what you feel, well, you stop feeling it.

She thinks how strange it is that she never had to struggle to find words to express her passion when she was first with Leo, though she might actually hate him now. And one of the things she hates him for is the fact that he unlocked that first rush of passion and there can only be one first love, one time when a monochrome world first explodes into colour. For Leo to be the recipient of that makes her feels like a victim of theft.

She puts her pen aside and picks up her sketchbook. Starts to doodle at first and then, a little to her own surprise, she finds she is drawing a face. Elli's face.

She works fast. It is an accurate portrait and full of love.

She is still working on it when Leo enters the room. She recognises his heavy tread, the way he disturbs the air in the room, stirs it somehow, but also chills it. A strange trick. He hovers at her shoulder, standing too close and breathing too noisily. She wonders at how easy it is to be irritated by those you used to love. Go past a certain point after an affair is over and literally everything they do annoys.

'The Finnish girl,' he says, though Rosa is aware he knows her name. 'It's a good likeness.'

Rosa doesn't respond, keeps working. This might be her best portrait yet. So often the mind and the eye can see the essence of a thing, but the hand can't follow it. Today it is different. Hand, mind, eye all working together: all have the same goal, speak the same language. It is a rare and precious moment. If she speaks, she could lose it. There is a triumphant heat building in her stomach. All art is a failure to a greater or lesser extent, but for once she feels a clear and definite success is possible. Right here at the end of her fingertips. Seeing how things really are and then revealing that so the world can see it, these are revolutionary acts, as important in their own way as writing a pamphlet or organising a strike.

Behind her she hears Leo's heavy breaths and, without warning, with one quick but deliberate movement, he has reached down, snatched up the book, torn out the page, ripped the image into pieces and let those pieces fall to the floor.

He places the sketchbook carefully, gently, onto her writing desk. He says nothing, but smiles slightly, nods and turns to walk to the door.

Rosa sits and looks at the sketchbook. She opens it to a new blank page, considers the annihilating flawlessness of the paper. She knows a true revolutionary would immediately begin again, would accept the setback as inevitable and something to be overcome with renewed effort, but she also knows that the effort is beyond her.

16

A High Diving Board

Dusk outside the Houses of Parliament. Koba and Elli Vuokko beneath a street light, moths feathering around their heads. The city's noises softened by the yellow fog that weaves itself around them. Elli reaches out a hand to touch the cool damp railings that surround the building.

'Can you believe we're here?' she says.

'London?'

'Yes, but not just that. That we're in London at this moment. This exact time of change and opportunity. That we're in the capital city of the most powerful country on earth at the dawn of the twentieth century, the start of a new era. You a shoemaker's son and me a factory girl and both of us from places no one's ever heard of. Speakers of languages unknown outside their own countries. Don't you think that's bizarre?'

Koba's face is a mask. He works hard to keep from sighing. Every generation feels that their time and place is special. He is somehow disappointed by the banality of her observation.

'Life itself is remarkable,' he says. 'Astonishing that anyone is anywhere.'

'That's true I suppose.' She turns away from him, holding the railings with both hands now as she gazes up at the Parliament building. The engine room of the British Empire.

He looks at her slender shoulders, her straight back, her neck pale beneath the heavy rope of her hair.

'My wife thinks everything is proof that there's a God. This city, this building, this light, these insects. The fact of us being here now, the mystery of it all. Even the system of government we live under, she would say that they are all proof of a divine creator.'

He can see Kato now, in their small kitchen at home staring at a cabbage, suddenly transfixed by all its veiny intricacies. He can hear her wondering aloud how could anyone look at something like this and say there is no God?

Probably a mistake to mention his wife. Maybe it will change the mood. Kill it completely even. But here is Elli turning back to face him smiling.

She takes his arm. 'Let's get away from the light.'

No need for him to worry. He had forgotten how ruthless young women can be in pursuit of their own desires. The fact he has a wife in Tiflis is not going to put her off, perhaps even makes him seem more desirable. It is possible.

They have been wandering the streets of London for hours now, striding away from the Brotherhood Church as if they had an important mission. They had left the East of the city for the West. Left behind the poor and familiar for the rich and strange.

He has enjoyed the attention they attracted from the people around them today. So many of these English drones so thin and exhausted. So many of them disfigured and weak. Koba knows that among these enfeebled citizens Elli and he make an exotic couple. The Viking girl with her extraordinary hair who moves with the loose, self-confident stride of a ballet dancer, restrained power in every step. The dark young man with the intense eyes and the boxer's swagger. Yes, he is wearing old clothes – a torn coat, a stained cap – but he knows he wears them well, that they flatter him more than a fine suit would. His ragged clothing makes him seem more dangerous, more devil-may-care than he is. There is a glamour in his kind of ugliness.

They have a copy of an old guidebook purchased for a penny at a bookstall. Following this they have been to the Tower of London, they have seen Buckingham Palace, they have walked over Westminster Bridge and back again. They have been to St Paul's and to some lesser known attractions too. They have been to the dog cemetery in Hyde Park and followed this by peering in the window of the barristers' wig shops in Lincoln's Inn.

He can't remember ever having had a more pleasant day.

Koba never did anything like this during his courtship of Kato. Despite her father's impeccable Socialist leanings, their romance had been conducted according to the strict rules of traditional propriety. Walks were always chaperoned by her mother or her grandmother. Time alone was snatched and fleeting.

Elli leads him away from the busy thoroughfare now, and they walk through College Green into the side streets around the Parliament buildings. Without talking about it they seem to have made a decision, seem to be looking for a spot that will give them privacy. A place to kiss and touch each other. Maybe more.

It's time.

'Where now?' says Koba.

'The guide recommends seeing the sheep kept in Green Park.' She pauses before quoting from the pamphlet in what seems to him like flawless English. '*It is a reminder of the countryside in the modern city.* We should go there.'

Sometimes Koba imagines that the whole world can speak English without thinking about it. The whole world except him. He has to think hard about it always.

'Is it far?'

'Not far.'

Yes, a park will be good. Pubs and parks, that's what London has. Places to drink yourself senseless for almost nothing and places to fumble with your girl out of sight. But perhaps he can do better than that?

He wonders about renting a room in a hotel. He can afford it after all, he's still hardly touched the Okhrana money. Giving Arthur money, his cutter, to purchase sweets has not made much of an inroad into it. And there is something glorious in the Tsar paying for him to find a place to screw. It needn't be a double cell in a fleapit like Tower House. It could be a clean place, somewhere with nice prints on the wall. He even has the money for a night in a place like Ulyanov's, a place where an obsequious clerk says 'Thank you, Sir' and 'Much obliged, Sir'. A place where he can take his time looking at her, all of her. Where he can take his time unwrapping her like a gift. Exploring her secrets as if she were a mansion or a private island. What is the point of the Okhrana money if he can't spend it?

He lingers on the idea for a few moments before dismissing it. It would lead to too many questions from his comrades. Maybe he and Elli could slip away from the conference again another day, or after tomorrow's salon at Joseph Fels' place. Or the day before they sail for home perhaps, there would be the added poignancy of parting that can make moments of love even sweeter, even more passionate.

Of course, he can't be sure that Elli will welcome the suggestion. He remembers the reporter outside the Worker's Club saying *it's all free love and nudism*. That hasn't been his experience, though it was true that the really committed Socialist girls never made him wait as long as Kato had. Her God had a lot to answer for.

He is aware of a pull at his arm.

'What are you thinking?'

He looks at Elli. Her face is worried. Determined, but worried. She is still so young. He needs to remember that. Her lioness ferocity is an act still being rehearsed.

'You must never ask a man that.'

'Why not?'

'Because he's not usually thinking anything. Or thinking something very dull, like what to eat or where his next drink is coming from.'

'Oh,' she says. She looks downcast. Perhaps he has spoken more harshly than he had intended.

She takes a visible breath. She smiles now, but bravely. She looks like a girl on a high diving board, a girl who has just walked up the steps with grace and bravado only to find courage evaporating now she's here, at the top.

Which is when he sees his father, large as life and lounging insolently across the street, hands in his pocket.

'I thought you might be thinking about sex,' says Elli.

'What? Sorry?'

Her expression has changed. Now she looks less like a girl on a high diving board and more like a girl about to undergo dentistry and the rest of her words come out in a rush. Not panicked exactly, but almost. She keeps her eyes on the pavement as she speaks, 'I thought you might be thinking about sex with me. About going somewhere hidden from view and touching me. Putting yourself inside me.'

Her eyes glance downwards at his groin. Then she shuts them for a moment, as if remembering something.

Her eyes open again. She stares down into his. How Koba

hates being shorter than a woman. It's wrong. It's against nature.

Elli takes another breath and when she speaks again, the nervousness is entirely gone. She's broken through some invisible barrier, to a place where the air is intoxicating, where she can say anything without fear. She is filled with exhilaration now. 'I was thinking about touching you.'

She is flushed, the way she is after the ju-jitsu sessions. Her eyes are bright. Her smile generous and wide. She is breathing rapidly. She looks beautiful, radiant. And still she has more to say, 'Or maybe you were thinking about getting a hotel room where we could do it properly, where we could take our time really getting to know each other. Where we could do it all night.'

Sometimes the telepathy of women astounds him. Their telepathy and their boldness.

London recedes. There is just this bubble, Elli Vuokko and Koba. No one else exists.

'You're blushing,' she says now. Was he? 'Yes. You're blushing and you're speechless.' She laughs.

Koba shakes his head. The bubble evaporates. London and all its busyness and bustle rushes back in on them. He turns to look at the people hurrying along the pavements, heads down avoiding eye contact, the groups of idle men, hands in empty pockets. The horses and the donkeys pulling carts. What should he do now? Should he laugh? Should he grab her and kiss her? Whatever is required of him, he doesn't feel able to do it.

He has avoided looking towards where his father is. He looks now. Just a quick glance. Yes, he's still there. A cut-paper figure, black against the deepening twilight. The old bastard.

'Don't talk like that,' Koba says.

Even to his own ears his voice sounds truculent. Petulant.

'Why not?' Elli's tone is still light. Her eyes shining, wide mouth still smiling but less brightly. The exhilaration is fading, stubborn bravery returns, determination returns.

'Because . . .' Because what? 'Because it's disgusting, because you are better than that.'

He feels like crying. He hadn't meant to say disgusting. He can feel tears welling but he also feels like starting a fight, feels like giving in to the sour and sudden rage beginning to burn in his gut.

Elli sighs, turns from him. He looks beyond her and across the street. His father has gone now. Of course he has. He has accomplished what he came to do.

'Men are so obvious,' Elli says after a moment. 'You're right, we never need to ask what you're thinking.'

Koba makes an effort now. Closes his eyes. Tries to swallow back the anger. Where does it come from, this desire to tear everything down?

'Don't be like that. It's just that you're wrong in this case. You're an attractive girl but I was thinking nothing like that,' he says. 'I was thinking we should get back to our respective lodgings. There is much to read before tomorrow.'

'I've frightened you.' Her voice rises, there is disdain in it too. 'Men are not only obvious but they're also timid. So afraid of women. So afraid of themselves around women. So horrified by the needs women bring out in them. So full of shame.'

He is dumbfounded.

She seems furious suddenly, moving away from him, disappearing into the yellowish haze of the London dusk.

'I will see you in the Brotherhood Church tomorrow, Comrade Ivanovich. Make sure you've done your homework. All that important reading.'

17

Mirror Gestures

A meeting room upstairs in the Rose Street Club. Ulyanov is briefing the delegates selected to attend the fundraising party. Six of the younger women, among them Elli Vuokko and her roommate Nina Kropin, and ten intellectuals. Nine men and Rosa Luxemburg.

'We are broke,' he begins. Ulyanov is calm, smiling even as he lays out the brutal truth of the financial situation. 'Flat broke. We have so little money that we cannot even afford to pay for all our people to get home from London. So, any cash we extract from our tame soap millionaire is our best chance of making a clean getaway.'

Ulyanov laughs at the groan this comment receives. He's been expecting it. His eyes twinkle behind his little round spectacles.

'Leave the jokes to Litvinov,' someone calls. 'Otherwise we'll definitely be coming away empty-handed.'

'We'll be arrested!' someone else shouts.

'And rightly so,' says another voice.

The chosen delegates are in a giddy mood. A party! A break from the debates, the arguments, the votes, the defeats. The endless useless talk. It will be good to have something nice to write home about for a change.

After a few more words from Ulyanov he gives the floor to Maxim Gorky. It was Gorky who had first made contact with the millionaire Joseph Fels during last year's profile-raising tour of the United States, Gorky who has the lowdown on him, who knows best how to approach him.

He begins by telling them what they already know: that Joseph Fels is an American industrialist, with homes in both the United States and England, and someone known to support progressive causes.

In quick, curt sentences he gives them the rest of his history. Born of German Jewish immigrants in 1853, by 1876 he had assumed control of a soap manufacturing company based in Philadelphia. In 1894 he developed that famous Fels-Naptha soap brand. This is a preparation, made in London but sold worldwide, that purports to help ameliorate any number of skin conditions including acne, psoriasis and dermatitis.

'You've all seen the British people up close. You've seen how much they need such a formula.'

He tells them that while building his own fortune very quickly, Fels has become an adherent of Henry George and his idea of the Land Value Tax, the so-called Single Tax.

'He is obsessed with it.'

'Who is Henry George and what is the Land Value Tax?' Nina Kropin whispers to Elli Vuokko. Elli shrugs, but Gorky is not pausing to take questions. He has moved on to telling them about how, seven years ago, Fels celebrated the dawning of a new century by helping found the Utopian colony of Arden, Delaware. A place run on strict Georgist principles – all land held in common, no private ownership. It's one of several experimental labour colonies he has funded.

'Of course, most of you will know George's book *Progress and Poverty*,' continues Gorky. 'But just in case any of you happen to be unfamiliar with his concept of the Single Tax, his belief was that the economic value derived from land, including natural resources, should belong equally to all members of society. Therefore a substantial levy should be imposed on those who wish to benefit from improvements made to it.'

There is a pause, a drink of water, a look around the room. Maxim Gorky is a veteran of a thousand book readings and knows how to engage an audience even when the subject is not immediately riveting. You need to keep your voice deep and low, you need to break your talk into manageable chunks, to leave some air between passages. Most of all, you must ensure you get proper eye contact with as much of your audience as you can. It helps if you are, as Gorky is, strikingly handsome. High cheekbones, thick dark hair growing low on his forehead, just enough streaks of grey to suggest experience, not enough to hint at decline. Sensual lips – almost too frankly carnal – shaped into the beginnings of a crooked grin, camouflaged by an untidy moustache. Eyes the colour of sunny early morning skies.

'You may think this is a naïve and simplistic view and one that does not account for the ruthlessness of landowners in defending rights of exploitation that they have achieved by force or by theft or by inheritance, but Joseph Fels is unshakeable in his conviction that the implementation of such a levy will, on its own, lead to a wondrous change in the fortunes of the working class. The thing to remember, to always keep at the front of your mind, is that Mr Fels is a major philanthropic supporter of many social reform projects including Socialist political parties, so we will not, on this occasion, be contradicting him. Not on the value of the Single Tax on land, or on anything else.'

'We will be dancing for treats,' says Litvinov.

'Just so,' says Gorky.

Another swallow of water, a little chuckle then he goes on to say that Fels may not be the only important target for the comrades tomorrow night. There will be other sympathetic industrialists with deep pockets. And there will be those, not rich in cash terms, but who have other kinds of capital, other kinds of power and influence. Some writers for example. H. G. Wells might be there, and if so, Comrade Bogdanov should definitely engage him in conversation, maybe get a few tips on writing successful science fiction ho ho.

Bogdanov remembers to laugh dutifully.

Gorky reminds them about the other useful idiots they might meet. Clergy, for example, maybe even a bishop or two. Oh, another thing to remember when talking to the host: Fels and his wife are Zionists. Last year Mrs Fels even undertook a trip to Mexico to investigate the possibilities of creating a Jewish homeland there. So there'll be some Jewish community leaders at the party. A nod towards the Jewish comrades in the room.

Several nods back. They know what to do.

The delegates are reminded that they should look out for politicians too. Joseph and Mary Fels are hoping that the Labour leader Keir Hardie will be there. There will be some representatives of the woman's suffrage movement. Maybe even Mrs Emmeline Pankhurst herself.

It's a good moment for Maxim Gorky to invite his companion Maria Andreyeva to the front.

Maria is keen to impress upon everyone there that this is first and foremost an acting job. They will be improvising the dialogue but that doesn't mean that there isn't a script to follow. That there aren't clear directions. No one should worry. It'll come naturally to most of them.

'Easy for her to say, she's a proper actress,' whispers Nina Kropin.

It's true, Maria Andreyeva has made a name for herself at the Moscow Art Theatre, has worked with Konstantin Stanislavsky no less.

Maria is convinced it is the Bolshevik women who will ensure success at this fundraiser.

'You are representative of a new class of women. A new breed. And you should flaunt that. Be loud, opinionated. Curse if you want. I assure you the bourgeois guests at this party will be enthralled. The wives especially will be thrilled by the sight of women talking freely and it is the wives that unlock the pocketbooks of their husbands. As for the unaccompanied men, well, we know what encourages a man to spend money.'

'We're not just dancing for treats, they're pimping us,' whispers Nina to Elli. 'Using our faces as bait.'

'Yes. Our faces, our bodies and our dirty mouths,' says Elli.

Maria pauses for a moment, lets them absorb the fact of their permission to be as uncouth as they like. When she starts speaking again it's to give them her Ten Rules for this event. One or two of the delegates reach for their notebooks. Maria shakes her head in amused irritation. No need to write this stuff down. Listen. Feel it.

She begins by telling them that the most important targets for the women are the group she calls The Tiaras.

'Rule number one: if you see a head wearing a tiara go for it, target it, talk to it. Pretend to yourself that you are the hostess and that your job is to make others feel welcome and at ease. Approaching a Tiara with this attitude will resonate.'

'And will you be wearing a tiara, Maria Andreyeva?' calls a voice.

Maria smiles. 'Of course, Comrade Litvinov. Tiaras are

for married women and, as you all know, I am a boring married lady.'

Laughter, scattered applause. Maxim Gorky colours a little but laughs along with the others. He and Maria have been together nearly five years now, but everyone knows that they are married already. To other people.

Maria Andreyeva holds up her hands for quiet. 'You need to listen for a bit longer,' she says. 'I have other rules.'

She tells them to stand tall. To pull their shoulders back and hold their heads high. 'That way you assume a posture of confidence and that's something that's attractive to men and women alike.'

She tells them to think about touch. Firm handshakes and light touches on the arm create a bond. But if you pull on people or touch them too often, you send unsubtle signals of desperation.

She tells them to use their bodies to show they're comfortable in the space. Suggests that they take an open stance with their legs a shoulder width apart and arms relaxed and loose at their sides.

'Don't cross your arms or use your drink or plate of food as a barrier. It makes you look walled off,' she says.

She tells them to mirror gestures. Her eyebrows arch as she realises that her audience are uncertain what she means. She sighs.

'When you subtly mimic the person you are speaking to, it is a way of silently saying that you're alike, that you share emotions, feelings, attitudes.'

She stresses the importance of making eye contact. She says that looking at someone's eyes conveys vitality.

'Notice the eye colour of everyone you speak with tonight, particularly the women, particularly the Tiaras. After a certain age no one looks into the eyes of women, so it is very seductive when it happens.' A pause. Another exaggeratedly meaningful glance at her lover.

Laughter.

She tells them that when they are in conversation, they should lean forward a little. 'It shows you're interested but,' a finger wagged here, 'also be mindful of personal space. In American business settings, even at a party, that means keeping at least ten vershki away. Some of you may struggle with this I know – and yes, I'm looking at you Comrade Litvinov. You too, Comrade Shaumian.'

More laughter.

She tells them to use open arm movements, to show the palms of their hands. Gestures like this will be seen as frank and persuasive apparently.

Her last rule is the most important rule of all. If they remember only one rule, they should make it this one: 'Smile. The human brain prefers happy faces. It rejects unhappy ones. If you smile, your target, your Tiara, will find themselves drawn to you. They will not be able to help themselves.'

'I'm not sure I can remember all that,' whispers Elli Vuokko to her neighbour.

'To be honest with you, I'm not even going to try,' replies Nina Kropin. 'I'm going to find my milord.'

18

The Real Enemy

The mansion on Park Lane is cool and smells of freshly cut flowers and money. The revolutionists queue to sign the visitor's book. They know the drill.

Most of the Socialists have been in houses like this before – some of them even grew up in this sort of luxury – but even those who have never been in regular contact with great wealth know that the ruling class sometimes like to have those who work for their destruction in to pirouette before them. They often like to believe that they are on the side of those on the margins. Sometimes, when discussing such matters among themselves, the party comrades wonder if it's a sexual thing, if the overlords are aroused by threat and danger, by a sense that they are vulnerable to violation by the exotic poor, by those who want them dead. Some put it more simply. It's a sexual thing yes, but that's because Socialists are just better looking than capitalists. It's a scientific, observable fact.

Others, more generous, say the thrill the rich get from mingling with Socialists is more like that of a fairground ride. It isn't really hazardous, but it feels like it is. Still others say that it's like a trip to the zoo for these people, that it resembles the pleasure of seeing lions and tigers close up, of witnessing the muscles in the shoulders ripple and knowing that the creature in the cage has the power to rip you apart and eat you.

The usual consensus, however, is that it's an exercise in power. The elite are so safe, so strong, so cocooned within walls of privilege, that they feel they can invite the monsters in with impunity. Not only that but they can make those monsters perform for titbits.

After Koba adds the name of Mr Ivanovich to the creamy pages of the visitors' book, he raises his head to take in the scene. The first thing he notices, as directed, are the tiaras worn by the older women, the way they glitter under the electric light of the chandelier, hard and sparkling indicators of status. The Tiaras are not his area, however, he can leave those to the women. He focuses instead on the formal suits of the rich men. The footmen impassive in their funereal black, hands moving quickly as they take the tall hats of the aristocracy, the bowlers of the bourgeoisie.

So far there are no ghosts. His dead father doesn't seem to be flitting around in the background, the way Koba had feared he might.

Koba sniffs at his glass suspiciously.

'What is this?' he asks Shaumian.

It is not Shaumian who answers, however. The plumply smug figure of Julius Martov has inserted himself into their group.

'It's called a daiquiri apparently. White rum and lime. A drink invented by the Americans after they conquered Cuba. To celebrate. There's also a champagne cocktail if you'd prefer, which is—'

'Brandy, sugar and champagne. I know, I'm not a barbarian.'

'Josef, you know we should be friends. If the party tears itself apart how can we expect to fight the real enemy.'

'Julius, I'm not sure you know who the real enemy is.'

There is a silence now, Martov sighs. Always performing,

thinks Koba, and right now he's performing disappointment.

'Look, whatever our differences, if ever you need my help, I will do all I can to be there. It's a promise.'

As Martov sails easily through the throng, shaking hands, smiling, radiating calm, quiet authority, Koba is left to wonder what the man knows. What has he heard?

Across the room, Elli Vuokko spies Koba. She thinks he looks surprisingly vulnerable in this arena. She closes her eyes, flushes at the memory of how forward she had been the previous night. How dismissive he had been in response, angry almost.

'Are you all right?' A soft, English voice. Upper class. Elli Vuokko opens her eyes. A young woman, maybe a few years older than herself is standing next to her with a concerned look on a pale, nervous face. There are grey shadows under her eyes, the hair is untamed, coming loose from the tie that keeps it back and off her face. It is not weighted down by any precious stones. She is manifestly not A Tiara, but perhaps she is someone Elli can practise her fundraising techniques on.

Elli smiles. Shakes the hand of her new acquaintance with careful firmness, makes sure she is not forming a barrier with her drink, wonders how to ensure that she shows her palms during however long this conversation is set to last.

She makes eye contact, tries hard to transmit energy and vitality, says that she's fine and asks, as a hostess might, her interlocutor's name, what brings her here and is she having a good time?

The new acquaintance maintains the eye contact – perhaps she has also had a pep talk from someone, has also been given a set of rules, perhaps she too is aiming to transmit vitality from her eyeballs – and tells Elli that she is called Sylvia, that she is an artist, a painter, and that she's here with her mother, and that yes, she's having a good time. She has already had two of these splendid cocktails and it settled her nerves rather. She tells Elli she is excited to be here amongst all these real live Communists because she has long been intrigued by the ideas of Marx and Engels. She asks if Elli is a member of the Russian Social Democratic Party.

'Yes, I'm a delegate from Tampere. Finland.'

'Finland! But you've just had elections. One where women were allowed to vote!'

Elli smiles. It is unforced this time, she doesn't have to remember to do it. Sylvia's reaction is so animated, it's like she's been given a sudden jolt of electricity.

'Yes, just a shame so many voted for the wrong parties. But perhaps it doesn't matter anyway.'

Sylvia frowns, 'Why not?'

Koba's words come back to Elli now: *The Diet itself is useless no matter how many women or proletarian representatives it has.*

She leans forward slightly: 'Just that parliaments rarely deliver real change. Transformation in societies happens first in the heart, then in the home, then in the streets.'

She finds herself worrying if she's ten vershki away from Sylvia. Maybe she should touch her shoulder? Or will that look desperate? She opts for smiling instead.

Sylvia returns her smile. Her whole face softens. She looks better now. Relaxed. She had looked rather tense before. Her face is definitely a happier one than it was at the start of the conversation. Elli warms to her more. Further proof that Maria Andreyeva's rules might actually be based on science.

'I think you should meet my mother.'

Sylvia points to where a severe woman in her early fifties stands in a small knot of people, all of them clearly listening to her with respect. And yes, she is wearing a tiara.

'You should introduce me.'

Which is how Elli Vuokko finds herself remembering to stand tall while she takes part in a spirited conversation with Emmeline and Sylvia Pankhurst about how the women of Finland have become the first in Europe to achieve the vote.

'Well, we had right on our side for a start—'

'But it wasn't that, was it?' Emmeline Pankhurst sounds amused, but Elli Vuokko notes that she doesn't bother all that much with smiling.

'No, we also used the threat that the revolution of two years ago would return.'

'Yes, winning the argument is one thing, but the threat of civil disorder also concentrates minds rather wonderfully. Of course Finland is not a sovereign state. Not a real country.' Again, another echo of Koba's dismissive words from a few days earlier. *The Diet is a house of paper. One strong gust of wind, one fart from the authorities, and it's gone.*

'Not an independent country yet. One day it will be. And when it is, it will be a Socialist one.'

Elli feels a touch on her arm. Sylvia. Yes, Comrade Andreyeva is right, gestures like this do create an instant rapport.

'Can I just say, you have an amazing face. I'd love to paint it one day.'

Elli knows what's going on here. The daughter is worried that the mother has been rude, that she has upset her daughter's new friend. It makes her feel even more kindly towards Sylvia. She knows that emotion. Her own mother is always saying things Elli thinks might upset her friends. Usually it turns out that her friends aren't offended, that they are surprised by the idea they could be, often they don't even notice her mother's crassness. If they do they tend to think

148

her mother's guileless insensitivity, her enquiries about her friends' love lives for example, are funny. Endearing almost.

How strange that Sylvia, like Rosa, wants to immortalise her in watercolours or whatever. Elli obviously has the kind of face that appeals to amateur artists. She can't decide if that's good or bad.

'That would be wonderful. Of course I am due home in a few days. Assuming we can get the money for the fare.'

Was that too gauche? Too obvious?

'I'm sure you'll be fine.'

Elli turns slightly to follow Sylvia's gaze. Sees Joseph and Mary Fels in animated conversation with Rosa Luxemburg, who is definitely remembering all she has been told about making connections. She is conscientiously leaning forward, touching the shoulder of Mary, the arm of Joseph, keeping her gestures open, her own arms loose, conveying energy through eye contact.

Elli wonders about the eye colours of Sylvia and Emmeline. Feels oddly panicked that she can't recall them.

'My friend Rosa is an artist too. Beautiful sketches of her friends.'

'I'm suspicious of Socialists who lose themselves in their own art. Suggests a dangerous self-absorption to me. The sin of Narcissus,' says Emmeline.

Elli notices how Sylvia's face seems to twitch.

It is at that moment that their little group is joined by a couple who Sylvia introduces simply as her friends Ramsay and Margaret from Leicester.

They seem pleasant, friendly, amiable but also utterly unimportant. Neither of them bothering to make themselves tall, to show their palms or anything. Margaret is not wearing a tiara and Ramsay is very definitely using his drink as a barrier.

149

Because they are so obviously irrelevant, Elli relaxes and finds herself having an interesting conversation about the National Women's Labour League. Margaret is fascinated by the idea that Elli is a lathe operator; she wonders how the Finnish men take to sharing factory space with female engineers. Margaret talks about the need not to alarm men while campaigning for votes for women and Ramsay talks earnestly about the need not to frighten middle-class voters if the progressives are ever to win a British election.

Elli laughs and says it strikes her that both men and middle-class voters deserve to be frightened, they need more fear in their lives, not less.

'They need to be panicked into sharing what they have.'

A footman brings drinks. As he moves away, she is surprised to find she has taken one. She takes a sip. Sweet. There is a hot glow in her stomach. When, a few moments later, the footman passes again, she takes another glass.

Is it her imagination or is the buzz of talk lessening a little now? Ramsay and Margaret say how nice it has been to talk to her, wish her luck with the rest of the conference and move away. Elli feels oddly bereft.

She feels this is something that was lacking in the preparatory talks Maxim Gorky and Maria Andreyeva gave before they came here. There needed to be a session on how to disengage from conversations. How to move away from them with grace and without anyone feeling bad. She remembers something her mother has always impressed on her: people don't remember what you say, but they always remember how you make them feel.

Time passes. Elli takes another drink. How many has she had now? Does it matter? No, she decides, it doesn't matter. She feels now that she might have been wrong about alcohol, might have simply been regurgitating the prejudices of her upbringing, which is a mistake for a Marxist. A good Socialist should always reason scientifically. She is looking around her for another Tiara –she feels ready to tackle them now – when she is joined by Rosa Luxemburg and two friends of hers. It is clear that Rosa has definitely decided it no longer matters how many cocktails they have. She sways slightly. Her eyes glitter, her skin shines.

The man is a leering type. His eyes fix on Elli's breasts as he shakes hands and they never leave save for brief excursions up to her neck before travelling back the way they came. He is obviously three sheets to the wind too. His companion seems bored, distracted, though perhaps it is just the way embarrassment manifests itself in her. Perhaps she is just tired. She's another using her drink as a barrier.

Rosa introduces them.

'Elli, I'd like you to meet Dr and Mrs Bunin. They are staying at the same hotel as Leo and I.'

By the time Elli and the Bunins have finished their how-do-you-dos, Rosa is excusing herself and disappearing into the crowd. Elli is irritated but also feels like laughing. So skilfully done. If they had had a session on exit strategies, they could have got Rosa to lead it.

It's only then that she remembers what Rosa had told her about this couple. Okhrana spies. Real live spies!

What a disappointment they are in the flesh.

Koba watches the Bunins lean into Elli Vuokko's personal space. What are they up to? He has been looking for an opportunity to talk to Elli himself but she has been surrounded all evening. First the suffragists, then Ramsay Macdonald and his wife.

Ramsay Macdonald might be the MP for Leicester, he

might be one of the twenty-eight Labour members of parliament elected last year, he might even be a leading voice among British Socialists, but he is hardly a real replacement for Keir Hardie. There's no question about it: the Bolsheviks have been pretty much snubbed by England's left establishment. No H. G. Wells here either, though Koba doesn't care about that.

Until this moment Koba has mostly followed Litvinov as he moved from group to group, smiling and nodding, feeling useless as the big man joked his way around the room, a story for everyone.

The people Koba meets as he and Litvinov move through the party, the things he hears: There is Mr John Redmond, the Irish nationalist who is much tickled by how the leader of the Bolshevik faction speaks English with a distinct Dublin accent.

'It's true,' says Litvinov. 'Comrade Ulyanov learned his English from an Irishman.'

There is Miss Harriette Colonso who has recently ruined herself organising the legal defence of the Zulu King Dinuzulu against charges of treason for conspiring in last year's rebellion over the imposition of the poll tax in Natal.

'Knobkerries against machine guns. Not so much a war as a cull,' Miss Colonso says. 'And the king wasn't even a party to the revolt but still they want to exile him, send him to St Helena as if he was Napoleon.'

There is a jolly little cherry-faced man, Mr William Greener, who is a gunsmith and inventor of the most efficient modern weaponry. 'I have recently had the honour of receiving the sincerest compliments from rival manufacturers, to wit the attempt to steal my designs and pass them off as their own. If you buy a decent gun in Europe chances are it will be a blatant copy of one of mine.' His chest visibly swells with pride as he says this.

'Fascinating,' says Litvinov. 'I have a professional interest in such things. We should talk more.'

But Mr Greener, the author of six books on guns, including the best-selling *Sharpshooting for Sport and War* is not interested in contacts in the armaments trade. Instead he is here primarily to find someone who will buy the dramatic rights to his novel *The Exploits of Jo Salis*.

'It's a story of British agents working for both sides during the recent Russian–Japanese war. I think you fellows would like it actually, but I feel a stage version could be arranged with strong heart interest, very strong heart interest. Just need the right young emotional actress.'

After he moves on towards more promising targets, Koba says, 'Why would an expert on guns want to write novels? Why swap a useful pursuit for something so trivial? And why would he think we'd be interested in such things?'

'No accounting for the mysteries of the human mind, my friend,' says Litvinov.

There is the corpulent Mr Henry Hyndman with his long mournful face and his extravagant beard, the man who came within 350 votes of winning the town of Burnley for the Marxist Social Democratic Federation in the last general election. Koba and Litvinov spend several unpleasant minutes listening to him blather on about the desire of Jewish capitalists to create a Hebraic Empire in Africa.

'And many of those capitalists are here! In this very room! Cooking up God knows what Machiavellian plans for the benefit of the Gold International!' Hyndman's voice is harsh and loud and Koba is nervous that their hosts will associate this anti-Jewish rhetoric with his own views.

He is relieved when, irritated at a lack of enthusiastic agreement, Hyndman moves on.

Litvinov is more relaxed. He smiles, chuckles for a

moment then says, 'Don't mind Henry. His problem is that he was a top sportsman in his youth and thinks political action is like a cricket match, one where he is the team's star player who gets to do and say whatever he likes and the rest of the team are there simply to lace his boots and applaud when he takes a wicket or hits a boundary.'

Koba wonders what the hell a wicket is and what it means to hit a boundary, but he's not going to ask.

Eventually they find their way to Joseph and Mary Fels where they endure a spirited session of agreeing with Joseph that the single Land Value Tax is indeed an idea of genius whose time has definitely come. Litvinov demonstrates his mastery of the art of sycophancy by playing the part of a sceptic gradually won over to the idea by the superior debating skills of Joseph Fels. He allows Fels to think he's made a convert. No one is more magnanimous, or more generous, than the man who thinks he has used his own wits to win an argument. And if that victory is against someone whose skill in debate is well known, whose intelligence is celebrated, so much the better.

Koba tries to play his part. Not in as grand a style, but when Mary Fels seeks his views on the possibility of a Jewish state, he agrees that such a thing is not only desirable but an inevitability. If not in Palestine, then somewhere else. Yes, Mexico is a good idea, but why not Russia? What do you think, Litvinov?

Litvinov is quick to agree, quick to assure Mrs Fels that there is plenty of support for such an idea in Russia, plenty of suitable land too. Rich farmland blessed with a temperate climate.

'Imagine a Jewish state run like the Arden Colony only on a vast scale,' he says. 'What a victory for progress that would be. And we can make it happen.'

Mary Fels looks at Litvinov with a face of such shining gratitude that Koba feels a stab of envy.

Now Koba finds himself on his own in this crowd. He looks around. There's Bogdanov glowering as cheerful conversation goes on around him. Clearly no one has recognised him or asked about his writing. Ulyanov is smiling so Koba imagines the central mission has been accomplished. He has the cheque, or the promise of one, in his jacket pocket.

Fels will be a man of his word. A promise delivered in this forum is one he will consider binding. Successful businessmen are like that. They will exploit their workers without mercy, rob their customers without thinking, but at the same time they'll be rigorous in honouring debts and promises to their peers. It's as if to rich people, only other rich people are truly real.

There is no reason for Koba to stick around. He will leave, make what Litvinov calls a French exit: one minute you're there, the next you're gone. No one sees you leave and you make sure you say goodbye to no one. It's always the goodbyes that take up a man's precious time.

He almost makes it, too. He gets as far as the door that leads to the hallway, when there is a hand on his arm. Elli. She is drunk and the look in her eyes is wild. For a moment he is sure that she is going to repeat her offer of yesterday, and this time he will accept with alacrity. Then he sees the truth. She is grabbing him out of quite another kind of desperation. So frantic is she to escape the soul-sucking embrace of the Bunins that she'll make a grab at anything, even him. Elli attempts an introduction, but Dr Bunin interrupts, 'But, my dear young lady, Mr Ivanovich and I are old friends.'

Koba thinks about denying that he has ever met the man, but quickly sees this would be a mistake. Any lies you tell should incorporate as much of the truth as possible. That is the first rule for anyone forced to lead any kind of a double life.

'We've met twice,' Koba says.

'In London yes, by happy accident in the street, you gave us recommendations for cheap places to dine, but my wife and I we are sure we know you from Moscow too. Or from Stockholm perhaps. I am sure we had a conversation where we agreed the Nordic countries were peculiarly unsuited for revolutionary activity, that it would be those of hotter blood, those from Southern climes, that would lead successful uprisings.'

'I don't think so.'

'I'm sure of it.'

A silent battle of wills, the air thickening around the four of them, before Mrs Bunin says in her flat, disassociated voice 'My husband may be mistaken.'

'Yes, yes, it's true that all you revolutionaries begin to look the same after a while. It's the faces. The same angry, bitter, joyless expressions. I'm afraid you rather blur into one another.'

Elli speaks now, 'Mr Ivanovich, will you please escort me to a place where I can get a cab. I find I have become rather unwell.'

It has been raining while they were inside the Fels house and a sharp ammonia scent rises from the streets. It sobers Koba, whose head clears as he holds Elli firmly by the elbow to move her away from the broad avenue of Park Lane and into one of the quiet streets nearby.

'I don't think we'll find a cab here,' says Elli, but there's a smile in her voice. Koba feels a sudden lightness of heart. He doesn't know why, but he is suddenly sure things – all things – might just turn out all right.

Elli hugs him and then stands back from him. She smells of champagne, cream and sweat. In her grey dress, in the wet dusk, she is beautiful but insubstantial somehow, like a ghost. She steps forward again.

'Sing,' she says.

'What?' he says.

'Sing to me.'

'Are you serious?'

'Yes,' she says. And he can see that she is. Maybe she wasn't when she first asked, but she is now.

'Sing what?'

'Anything.'

'I can't.'

'You don't know any songs?'

He does know some songs. Quick now! she is turning away. She is moving down the street, her step light. The blood twists through his body. He begins. He sings *Mravaljamier*, Forever More. Softly, but insistently. Just a minute or so.

She turns back to face him, steps closer to him. Her eyes are wide. He raises his voice. As he sings his eyes fill, it gets hard to see Elli, he can feel the wetness on his cheeks. It is a song every Georgian child knows. Ancient, its author lost to history, a song about the duty of every person to be happy, to seize every opportunity to enjoy life, and a song that reminds the listener that only by being kind can you defeat evil.

An exquisite lie.

He falls quiet after a few verses. They stand in silence, a silence somehow enriched, more thickly textured, because of Koba's song. There are playful notes that linger, that creep into nooks and corners of the street.

'Beautiful,' she breathes at last. 'Beautiful.'

'You need at least three voices to sing it properly. That's what Georgian music is, a chance to blend different voices – many souls all singing separate parts, all making a powerful single piece.'

'It's like how the world should be.'

She puts her arms around him. He can feel her heart dancing beneath her breasts, feel the rise and fall of her breathing, smell the heady scent of her.

'The strange couple we met before we left the party? Rosa says they're spies.'

'Of course they're spies.'

'But they know you.'

'And now they know you. Everyone in the party knows spies. It would be suspicious if you didn't.'

She thinks about this, seems to accept it.

'Why didn't you make love to me last night?'

'Because I am a fool.'

Now he pulls her in close to him, bends to kiss her, and finds himself hitting the ground with a hard thump. He is on his back looking up at a clear sky, the bats that flicker around the rooftops. An owl calls from somewhere. His breath has gone. He feels nauseous, lies back in the road. He'll wait until the sickness passes.

He can hear Elli laughing but from this position he can't see her. He hears her footsteps skipping away from him. He raises himself up on his elbow.

'We're even now,' she calls over her shoulder. 'We can start again.'

19

Maybe It's For The Best

The men in this room are lapping at their cups with enthusiasm. Maybe it's because the tea is thick, brewed in a proper samovar, or because the sugar is cut from a proper loaf. Everyone is making smacking noises with their lips. The brew is much needed, as they all seem to have a thirst and a sore head. Some have picked up mysterious injuries. Mikhail Tskhakaya in particular looks terrible. His skin is a chalky grey, his eyes are red and there's a light gloss of sweat across his forehead. He holds his tea cup with both hands, sniffs constantly. Coughs.

Koba rubs at his hip. He's also in a bad way. There is an ugly bruise the size of a saucer there beneath his trousers. Every time he thinks about how he got it, his guts shrink a little. At least there were no witnesses to his dishonour. Maybe it can just be forgotten about.

Koba, Yanofsky, Litvinov, Bogdanov, Tskhakaya, Gorky and Shaumian are gathered in Ulyanov's rooms in Gray's Inn Road and the only person who doesn't look like he's sickening for something is their host. On the contrary he is in a cheerful mood. Teasing. Tongue flicking over his lips from time to time, a playful lizard. Ulyanov tells them that he has good news and he has bad news, asks which they would like first. Koba suggests they go for the bad, but he is outvoted.

'The story of your Congress, old friend,' laughs Litvinov.

So, Ulyanov starts with the good news which is that Fels has come through with a promise of $7,500.

'And the bad news?' says Koba

'He wants it back in a year. With interest. This is very much a loan not a gift.'

Ulyanov tells them that he made the Bolshevik leadership sign a document. They are legally obliged to repay.

'Bastard,' spits Bogdanov.

'We can't complain, can we? It'd be like complaining about the weather, or about nature. Snakes bite, scorpions sting, capitalists lend money at interest.'

Litvinov wonders when they started being so conscientious about legal obligations. Ulyanov explains that they might want more money from Fels in the future – potentially quite a lot more – so best to fulfil the terms of this loan to be in a better position to renege on future loans if they need to.

'Cunning,' says Litvinov.

'You know the old saying that when it comes time to hang the capitalists, they will sell us the rope? Well, first they will lend us the money we use to buy that rope.'

Koba has had enough of all this pointless chatter.

'What do you want us to do?' he says, though he has an idea that he knows already.

'We need an expropriation,' says Litvinov

A noisy pause. The sound of tea being swallowed. Laboured breaths. Tskhakaya blows his nose.

'We do,' says Ulyanov.

He refills his cup at the spout of the samovar, cuts himself some sugar. Holds it between his teeth in the old style as he swallows. Turns to Koba and, with his mischievous eyebrows twitching, with his neat beard waggling, asks him mildly if he has any ideas.

'You put him on his arse with ju-jitsu? That's hilarious.'

Rosa Luxemburg and Elli Vuokko are in the Haggeston Baths again, wreathed in hot steam again. Voices of laughing women echoing off the tiles again. Smell of cheap soap again. From here Elli can see a spider's web with a fat fly struggling in it. A few inches away she can see the spider herself, waiting until the struggles stop.

She lathers her feet and legs, then drops the soap into the water, watches as it grows clouded and milky.

'What happened?'

'I'm not sure,' Elli says. She closes her eyes, lies back against the enamel of the bathtub, feels the water supporting her gently, her skin at one with it. She can't tell where her body ends and the water begins. She feels permeable. As if she is slowly and pleasantly disintegrating, merging into the water like the soap. She doesn't even care if her hair gets wet today. Maybe she'll get it cut. A proper revolutionary act.

She pictures herself stumbling from the house in Park Lane. Koba pulling her down a side street, Koba singing! Singing because she asked him to. Then his face looming up into hers, his hands on her shoulders, breath smelling of brandy and champagne. His lips, the rough tickle of his moustache against her chin and then his tongue and that's when she did it, pulled him close against her as he leaned in then twisted from her hip so, already unbalanced, Koba had gone over like a felled tree.

The feeling of liberation and triumph as she had walked back to the broad sweep of Park Lane and summoned a cab.

'Mrs Garrud would have been so proud of you,' Rosa

says, breaking into her thoughts. 'She said you were good right from that first lesson. What happened next?'

'Nothing,'

'Really? The sensitive Koba took rejection lying down?'

'He didn't have much choice.'

Rosa laughs politely.

Had that been the end of it? Hard to remember. Had she given him a piece of her mind? Had she told him that he'd had his moment and he'd blown it. People – men – got one chance with Elli Vuokko and if they passed it up, then it was their loss. No way back.

Had she actually said all this or just imagined that she had? She hoped she'd said it.

She can't remember getting home, though there's a vague almost-memory of a horse whinnying, a cab driver complaining about the traffic, making small talk about the weather, expressing the hope that she doesn't puke in his cab, then nothing until she woke fully clothed, throat and mouth so dry that her teeth felt too big for her, wondering where her roommate Nina was.

'Well, he's an idiot anyway.' Rosa's tone is emphatic. 'Maybe it's for the best.'

After this a quietness falls between them. They listen to the voices, to the splashing. Such a happy, innocent place this world of women. And spotless, smelling of vinegar as well as soap. A sanctuary. A place untainted by dirt or by men. Even that spider is helping keep things clean. One of the first lessons Elli remembers her mother teaching her is that spiders are ugly, but they are your friends. They catch and kill the bugs that spread infection.

Elli thinks about Nina, about how she had walked back into their room in the early morning just as Elli was setting off for the baths. She was keen to share the adventure of her night, to tell Elli about spending it in the Fels' mansion, sharing a hard, narrow bed with one of the footmen.

'Shameless aren't I?' she'd said, laughing. 'Not exactly a milord. Still, I think I made a convert to the revolution and I didn't have to shoot him afterwards.'

Nina told Elli that just an hour earlier that footman had asked her to marry him, which was at least a sign that she'd made an impression.

'What did you say?' Elli had asked.

'I said maybe I would. Said I'd think about it anyway.'

'I hope—' Elli had begun.

'Yes, yes, yes. I was careful. He didn't get to spend inside me. I made him do it across me not in me.' She laughed. 'I wasn't that drunk. I kept my head screwed on.'

How casual other people could be, thought Elli then. How easy they could be about things.

'This is nice,' says Rosa at last. Elli, her eyes still closed can hear the slosh and slap of the water as her friend sits up suddenly, a thought seeming to occur to her. 'I owe you an apology I'm afraid,' she says.

'Do you?'

'Yes, for abandoning you to the Bunins.'

'It's all right.'

'No, it's not. They are boring and they are annoying. The husband particularly. At breakfast every morning there they are, asking if they can join me at my table. Doesn't matter what time I get up, doesn't even matter if I am obviously trying to read, or to write a letter.'

'Funny. They know Koba too.'

They lapse back into silence, but not for long. Rosa is in a talkative, flighty mood. And no wonder. It is her last full day in London. She is all packed, ready to go back to Berlin. Leo is staying in London for another day or so, she'll be free

163

of him, at least for a while. Free of his whining and his sulking and his threats to do violence to her or to himself. She'll be able to spend time planning how to manage a final break with him. To find a way of making sure he knows that things are definitely over between them. And of course she can spend a day or two in bed with Kostya.

As Rosa talks Elli allows her thoughts to drift. She thinks of everything and nothing. How everyone and everything seems connected. About how the world is shrinking all the time. Tampere, Moscow, London, Berlin all connected by the telegraph, the post and the telephone. She thinks too of how small concerns keep tugging human actors away from any grand plans they have. A world revolution is a big thing. Sleeping with Koba or not, Rosa discarding her lover to replace him with a boy – these are tiny, inconsequential matters. Yet the big things are often eclipsed by the effects of the most trivial events.

Maybe Nina's footman will end up doing some marvellous dramatic revolutionary act, something that changes everything, that shifts the world on its axis – just to demonstrate his love for her. Perhaps he'll shoot a king, blow up Parliament or something. You could hope for that, but probably the opposite would happen. It's more likely that Nina will be lost to the cause because one night she doesn't keep her wits about her. One night she'll be too drunk to think, and that night the footman will spend himself inside her rather than across her belly. Then she'll be having babies in Whitechapel, with no time to think about anything else.

Her glance takes in the web again. The fly has stopped moving. Another battle in an eternal elemental struggle coming to its inevitable conclusion. The powerful crushing the weak. The cunning trapping the unwary. The world divides into spiders and flies in the end, and the battles will always end the same way until the flies can surpass nature, until they can make webs of their own.

'They're very poor secret agents, aren't they?' Rosa says.

'Who? The Bunins?'

'Yes, they're so feeble that I think the real agents must be elsewhere, somewhere in the shadows, laughing because they know everyone at the Congress is nudging each other, thinking they're being all so very sharp-eyed and clever as they point out the comical decoy agents to one another. The real spies will be like the invisible man.' She thinks for a moment. 'Or maybe they won't be in the shadows. They'll be very visible, they'll be in plain sight. They'll be people we trust completely.'

'Do we trust anyone completely?'

'We shouldn't.' She hears the gurgle and swish of the water as Rosa wriggles in her tub. 'But sometimes we can't help ourselves. Anyway, this time tomorrow I'll be in Germany! Or almost. On the way at least.'

As they return to the lockers where they left their clothes, Rosa tells Elli she has something for her. Something to remember her by. From her bag she takes out a small picture sketched in ink.

'It's Mimi,' she says. 'The closest thing to a child I will ever have.'

'She's beautiful,' says Elli.

Rosa laughs as she admits: 'I was intending to draw you my dear, but I didn't have the skill.' She doesn't want to talk about Leo and the casual, furious destruction of her portrait of her friend. 'Whereas Mimi. Mimi's features are etched in my mind.'

'She has an unforgettable face,' says Elli.

'We must write to each other often,' says Rosa.

'We must,' Elli agrees.

20

Armour

Koba is waiting for the arrival of the Bunins in The Clive of India. Another public house that stands as a monument to a butcher. When they're not naming their pubs after mythical creatures, the English are naming them after killers.

It is busy today, full of red-cheeked men in despair. They don't express this by weeping but by talking at each other. Loudly. Koba can't understand many of the individual words but the sense is clear to him: *I said to him, I told him, I set him straight, he won't do that again in a hurry.*

Men complaining, bragging, carving a few moments from the evening in which to try and convince themselves that they are the heroes of their own story, when the truth, which, deep down, they must realise, is that they are not even bit part players. If life is a game of chess then most of these men aren't even pawns, they're not even on the board. For most working men, the dream of becoming a pawn is an impossible one. They know it; they can't admit it. To acknowledge it would destroy them.

The smoky gloom of the pub is in contrast to the world Koba has left outside. There it is a day of restless sunlight and small speeding clouds, a breeze stirring the leaves on the thin branches of the stunted trees that defy the damaged air of the streets.

Koba prefers it in here. The sunlight of the outside world

is too bright, too much like the light of the interrogation room. Here, where colour has died, he has found a cave, a place to hide, and the braying of the other men in here is another screen between him and the world.

A shield. Armour.

He sits for a few minutes more remembering his first encounter with the Okhrana more than six years ago. A police cell in Tiflis. His arrest for the illegal distribution of leaflets attacking the leaders of the Social Democrats in the city. He wasn't to know then that these leaflets, given to him by his friend Lado, were themselves part of an Okhrana provocation. The leaflets had been written by a police copy-writer, the underground press that had printed them was a police business. Many of Koba's fellow distributors were actual police operatives too. The Okhrana in Tiflis had real entrepreneurial flair when you thought about it.

The rhetoric in the leaflets was fierce, speaking of the lack of militancy at the top of the party, accusing them of betraying the proletariat, urging the workers to rise up and remove the lickspittle weaklings who were selling them out through their inactivity and lack of backbone. If all went well the workers would do as asked and leave vacancies at the top of the opposition forces for Okhrana agents to step into. Oh, the fun the police must have had writing that stuff. What innocent joy.

The operation was a rogue one, sanctioned by Captain Samedov, a senior officer in Tiflis whose second distribution of leaflets called for an uprising against the authorities in defiance of the caution of the left-wing leadership in the city. When Samedov's bosses in St Petersburg heard about it, they feared this provocation would work too well. That it would not result in the weakening of the top strata of the party, but might actually achieve its supposed aims, threatening the position of the authorities. Intended as a kind of vaccine, it might just accelerate the course of the Communist infection through the population instead.

Everyone involved in the leaflet campaign was arrested – innocent patsies and established provocateurs alike – and Koba quickly discovered the way he had been used. The authorities in turn had expressed their admiration for the efficiency with which he had conducted his part in the operation, had told him how impressed they'd been with his obvious intelligence.

Not that they told him this straightaway. No, first they let him stew in prison for a while, let him sweat in the company of the real hard men of the proletariat: the thieves, the bandits, the violators of women, those so sunk into degradation that they would rob priests and nuns before offering him a route away from the prison system. A path that could help them both. The chance to run some provocations of his own, the opportunities for promotion within the party that might come from the timely arrest of alternative candidates for leadership. The exchange of cold hard cash for information given at the right time. They had introduced him to Kamo, a petty thief with the swagger of a mob leader. An audacious but disorganised bank robber.

'He is a lunatic,' the police captain had said. 'But he's our lunatic. We think you'd make a good team.'

It has been a series of sordid little transactions ever since and has grown more dangerous with every passing year.

It is time to end it. Time to escape the Okhrana clutches while he still can. Let's get this over, he thinks. He will tell them he's out. They can do their worst.

Still, it is with reluctance that Koba moves from the public to the saloon bar. He has a sense of leaving home somehow.

There is despair in the saloon too but it is quieter, masked because of the presence of women. The room is much brighter too, with the light streaming through large, undraped windows.

The Bunins are in good form. Dr Bunin is almost sober, his work-wife is almost cheerful. They are going home.

'We have made your report for you, written the irrefutable evidence in the form of a letter that will reveal the spy who has been working for the Tsar all this time, the one who has been giving vital information that has resulted in the deaths of many comrades and the arrest of many others. Irrefutable evidence that will mean that your leadership team have to act or look ridiculous. A detailed note written in a difficult but breakable cypher and intended for the MO5, our close partners in the fight against international communism, thus proving this man will give the party up not just to the Russian ruling class but to foreign powers. Wickedness on a truly epic scale.'

'It is a man then.'

'Yes, it is a man,' says Mrs Bunin. 'No woman has yet risen to a position in the party where she is worth destroying. We considered Rosa Luxemburg. We did think about Maria Andreyeva, too, but in the end we decided they were ornamental rather than integral to the party's functioning.'

Dr Bunin is irritated by this interruption to his flow. His leg twitches impatiently, he drums his fingers on the table. 'If I may continue?'

Koba shrugs.

'Thank you.' A brief pause for the man to pick up his thread. 'Our report on the whole affair has made our time here seem exciting, important, necessary. You know how it is. You know what management likes.'

Koba does indeed know how it is. He does indeed know what management likes.

The couple are looking at him, expectant. What do they want? Praise? Applause? Do they really need his validation?

'You haven't even told me who I'm revealing as the traitor.'

Dr Bunin claps his hand to his head theatrically. 'Good heavens how silly of me.' He taps out a little paradiddle on the table. 'It is ... Meir Henoch Wallach-Finkelstein. Also known as Papasha. Also known as—'

'Litvinov! Are you crazy? No one will believe it. Everyone loves him.'

'They'll believe it. The more outrageous the lie, the more people want to believe it. The more outlandish the accusation, the more people will spread it around. And even if they're saying that they, personally, don't believe it, the mere act of passing the falsehood around gives it currency. In a world where everyone is paranoid it doesn't take much to unnerve people. Especially after Azef.'

The woman speaks now. 'It is the fact that everyone respects Litvinov that makes him such a good choice as our traitor. The revelation that he's a turncoat will shake the party, will make them distrust surface charisma and easy charm.'

Koba thinks of last night's party, of the guests that Litvinov had made feel a little more special by including them in the warm embrace of his bonhomie. The people who had felt a little more loved, a little brighter, by being in his presence. He wonders what they will say to one another after Litvinov is unmasked as a traitor. What kind of frisson will they get knowing that, a day or two after they were laughing at his jokes, he was efficiently murdered. John Redmond in Ireland, Harriette Colonso all the way out in South Africa. William Wheeler in his Birmingham gun shop, maybe turning the story into the plot of a new romance.

Hyndman shaking his head about it in his party office. All of them telling their acquaintances how they knew the dead Russian, chatted with him just recently, how he'd seemed like such a rakish, affable fellow, had seemed so straightforward, such good company. Just shows you never can tell. He thinks of Mary Fels' shining, hopeful face and immediately afterwards imagines the horror of Litvinov joining the ghosts that peep at him from the shadows, that frown at him at the edge of his vision. That will no longer be confined to dreams.

Will a dead Litvinov be content to keep to the dark spaces? Will he not instead follow Koba wherever he goes? There will be nowhere safe.

Bunin's partner cuts into his thoughts, 'The party's grim grey men suddenly fashionable, suddenly necessary. It will be important to be steady, almost invisible. This could be your time, Mr Ivanovich.' Dr Bunin claps his hands together. 'God, I'm looking forward to being out of this dreary place. I swear London is the sphincter of the world. Dark, dank, damp, smells of shit.'

He raises his glass to his lips, swallows.

'So, what happens?' says Koba

The plan, such as it is, is childishly simple. Some time tomorrow, incriminating documents will be placed in Litvinov's lodgings. Soon after, tipped off by Koba, Ulyanov will have the room searched and will find that one of his most trusted lieutenants is offering the embryonic British Secret Service details of Bolshevik movements as well as a list of party members who already act as informants for the Okhrana. A coup for their British friends, and, just possibly, a way of ensuring that they get voted a decent budget by a Liberal government suspicious of increasing police powers.

'You'll have been reading in the papers how we're working together closely these days, the British and us? They are more interested in the Germans of course, but I think we're persuading them that the threats to the established order are global now. The people named in the letter are real informers, by the way. Lowlife scum who have served their purpose and whose work for the Tsar will be easily proven. Expendable resources. Their loss will save the exchequer a few roubles a month. Litvinov will bluster and rave and then he'll disappear and no one will speak of him again.' A thought strikes Dr Bunin. Seems to tickle him. 'Do you think you might be tasked with ensuring the disappearance really is final? After all, you've done that job before.'

He had. An expropriation in Batsumi. The counting of the money, dividing it up among Kamo's criminal friends, the hoodlums who assisted with such operations at that time. The discovery next day of cash missing from its hiding place. Sums not adding up. A culprit unmasked. A Court of Honour convened in haste. The snivelling denials of the thief. What was his name? Davit something? Davit Ivanishvili? Something like that. His blubbering as sentence was passed. Koba choosing a young comrade to do what everybody agreed had to be done.

Comrade Akaki Gotsridze. Just fifteen years old, a boy who needed to prove himself. He was to take the rat out to sea, take care of things there and heave the body overboard. The discovery several days after the sentence was carried out that the supposed thief was innocent, the money had been found. The extravagant relief of Gotsridze.

'I can confess it now,' Gotsridze had said. 'The thief – the man we thought was the thief – he begged for his life. Told me about his wife and young family. Swore over and over that he was not to blame. And . . . I let him go. He agreed never to return to Batsumi or contact anyone from the party again, and I let him swim to the shore. Thank God.'

Poor, innocent Gotsridze. The sap had looked around happily at the faces of his comrades. The idiot had even looked puffed up, pleased with himself. As if he'd done a good thing.

Koba had known what to do then. Had taken care of it. Called on Gotsridze in the early hours with Kamo and a couple of others. His companions had knocked the boy unconscious and stood back while Koba put a bullet right between the eyes. Then they had watched while Koba took his father's old thick-bladed half-moon knife, the one he used for cutting tough leather to make sturdy boots, watched as he dug through the flesh and tissue of the kid's chest. Dark blood up to his elbows. The group had looked on, silent, spellbound, while Koba bent ribs so that he could saw through the sinews and tendons that held the heart in place, until he had that slippery organ in his hands. How light it was! And really no different to that of a pig or a sheep. The heart of a man is nothing really. The heart of a child, even less.

He hadn't enjoyed it. It had been a necessity though, everybody agreed. The boy had been given a job to do – an important job – and he hadn't done it. He had pretended he had, had deceived his comrades, had put his own squeamishness before the good of the party. It didn't matter that there had been no crime: at the moment he had let the traitor go he believed there had been. How could anyone trust him after that? And taking the heart, well, that sent a message. One that everyone heard.

Do something like that once and maybe you won't ever have to do it again.

Koba wonders what became of that heart. He had taken it to the next meeting. Had shown it around. Had made sure

173

everyone held the rotting, stinking thing in their own hands, but what had become of it after that?

Koba had expected to feel some profound change after that day. Surely, taking a life – cutting out a young heart – surely meant that you were forever altered? But it turned out that it was like losing your virginity. Changed nothing. It left no scars, no marks at all. Not at first. Not until the dead started gawping at you in parks. And you could get used to that easily enough. You can get used to anything.

He looks around the drinkers in the pub. Reminds himself again that being pestered by the dead is not so bad. Most people you meet are dead. They are just pretending to live. Sleepwalking through their lives.

'I still think you need more,' he says now.

'Yes, it would be good to have more but that's the trouble with framing the innocent, there's often a dearth of decent compromising material.'

'I have more you can use.'

The Bunins glance at each other. The woman sighs. It is clear they would prefer it if their work was done, finished. They don't want their good ideas killed by better ideas, don't want anything to add to their workload. They are sloppy. They are careless. They are lazy.

Fuck them. He's going to make them work.

Koba tells them about the next expropriation, the biggest there has ever been. A robbery at the Tiflis Central Bank and that Litvinov was there when the plan was being put together, so it will be easy to finger him for leaking details and have they got a pen between them because here's what you need.

They assure him that they'll remember. That they are trained for this.

Koba snorts at the idea that they are trained professionals. Nevertheless, he begins to give them the specifics. The who, what, where and when. The how. Exactly as he had laid it out earlier in Ulyanov's sitting room.

Dr Bunin stops him after a few moments. 'There is too much. We don't need the entire timetable.'

His voice has the petulance of a child who finds he has homework to do on the first day of a holiday.

Koba doesn't reply immediately. He waits. Silence, like keeping your contacts waiting, like having the firmest handshake in greeting or departing, is an effective weapon in destabilising your opponents.

'It's all right, my dear. I'll remember it all,' Dr Bunin's wife, colleague, companion, whatever, sounds both exasperated and amused. Oh, you men, her tone seems to say. Oh, your childish games. So typical. So silly.

When he finishes, there is a silence.

'This will definitely happen?' Dr Bunin sounds sceptical.

Koba doesn't answer this. Instead he complains about their recklessness, their unprofessionalism, their lack of respect. He does this in terse sentences.

'If the expropriation is called off, it will be because you have brought suspicion on me.'

He means their talking to him in the street, their arranging to meet him in public. He means their turning up at the house of Joseph Fels. Their talking to Elli Vuokko.

'Oh, now we get to the heart of it,' says Bunin. 'You think we have spoiled the possibility of a little romance with the fiery Finn.'

'Miss Vuokko came away from the party suspicious of you, which makes her suspicious of me. Which makes your work harder and puts my life in danger. I can't have that.'

'Is she suspicious of us?'

'I think anyone who sees the way you operate would quickly become suspicious of you.'

'Thank you for your observations and your insight, Mr Ivanovich. I am sure we're grateful for anything that helps us to become better at what we do.' The work-wife is both thoughtful and irritated. Koba has completely punctured their holiday mood. Good.

He is seized by a sudden weariness. The mention of Elli's name has brought with it a sadness. Would he always be afflicted by an urge to possess what he finds beautiful and, in possessing it, destroy what's good about it?

He thinks of Kato and Yakov, the son he's hardly met. Kato who is so frail, who worries so much about the state of Koba's soul. Now he's responsible for casually delivering one of his few friends into the hands of torturers and murderers. If there really is an afterlife, a Heaven and a Hell, then he has done himself no favours.

He smiles.

'I don't see what there is to smile about,' says Dr Bunin. He takes his little round glasses off, rubs at them with his shirt tail.

'I am smiling because I assume that not only is this the last time we meet, it is the last time I will ever work for the Okhrana.'

The Bunins look at one another and grin. For the first time they look like they might have been lovers once. Friends at the very least. For the first time, you can see that they have some kind of genuine bond.

'Absolutely fine,' says the Doctor.

'You're free,' says his wife.

The two of them exchange another look and they laugh.

'Unless your country needs you.'

'Unless there is a national emergency.'

So he learns what in his heart he has always known. His country will always need him, there will always be a national emergency. He won't be free of the Okhrana and all its Bunins until Russia itself is free of them. Until the Tsar is dead and his acolytes and servants destroyed or scattered. Until there is a final reckoning.

'Let us buy you another drink,' says Dr Bunin. 'You've more than earned it.'

21

The Hungry Light

The following evening, Koba wanders through the city, drinking the heavy London ales in crowded pubs, watching the tired, bitter working men try to forget their cramped lives. Trying to lose themselves in booze and big talk.

In the Cumberland Hotel in Old Kent Road, he looks up to find Stan, the little fixer from Tower House, standing in front of him. His quick, intelligent face is even thinner than Koba remembers. His manner even more solemn.

They nod at each other. It is Koba's way never to show surprise and the boy understands this.

'It's you,' says Stan, eventually.

'It's me.'

'I have a message for you.'

The message is that it's done. Hidden in Litvinov's effects in Tower House is a letter, in English and typed on the same make and model of typewriter that Litvinov owns, suggesting that, for a modest fee, he might provide useful information to the British Intelligence Services. A letter that provides as references the names of high-ranking officials of the Okhrana who will be happy to vouch for him and includes with it, a list of names of other people whose information the British can rely on. As further evidence of his good faith the letter also gives details of the planned Tiflis robbery. The planting of this letter was done by Stan himself, in a new false bottom of Litvinov's trunk. A hiding place constructed while the target was in the Brotherhood Church losing votes on the need for violent direct action.

'The people who employed you, do you do much work for them?'

Stan shrugs. 'I've worked for them before. I work for anybody.'

'You're good at the work?'

'I'm good at everything I want to be good at.'

Koba nods. He approves of this lack of false modesty.

'And your employers, the people who sent you to find me with this message, they pay well?' Koba finds that he has a need of company, that he doesn't want this conversation to end.

The boy shrugs again. 'To be honest with you it's not the earning, it's the investing that's important. Every penny I get from people like them, I put to work for me somewhere else.'

Encouraged to sit and drink a small glass of porter, Stan tells Koba his dreams of entering the rentier class. At present he can only dabble in moneylending but one day, well, you just watch. There'll be a big house in Kent, another in the West End. Horses. A carriage. Motor cars.

'And servants?'

'Yes, servants. Of course. Butlers and under-butlers. Even the under-butlers will have under-butlers of their own. Maids too, of course. Lots of those. And cooks and footmen. Someone to wipe my bloody arse for me. And when I'm old I'll be in the House of Lords and I'll make everyone in England do what I tell them. I'll have a coat of arms and everything.'

'And will you be a Liberal or a Conservative?'

'A Liberal of course.'

'Of course.'

They sit quietly for a moment. Stan perhaps lost in thoughts of future grouse shoots and coming out balls. He takes a sip of his drink and leans forward, elbows on the table. He's back in the room once again. A practical man of business making conversation with a client.

'Is your friend in trouble?' he says.

'He's in the kind of trouble that soon passes.'

'Oh dear,' says Stan. 'I liked him.'

'We all did,' says Koba and, after a brief pause, 'Tell me Stan. Where can I get one of those birds that you teach to sing?'

If it's going to be done, it has to be done quickly. What if Litvinov discovers the evidence? What if something makes him check his trunk for tampering? What if Stan is not quite as competent as his confidence suggests?

Koba moves through the London streets impatiently. His shoulders are tense, his damaged leg is starting to ache, the bruise on his hip is giving him grief, his jaw is set, his teeth are clenched, his hair is wild and his eyes flash. He pushes past anyone who gets in his way and some jostle him back and some shout crude remarks and others yell threats, but he's not deflected. He doesn't slow his pace.

When he reaches Ulyanov's place, he is breathless and takes a moment to look around him as he is ushered into the leader's presence, a few seconds to reset himself, to gather his thoughts. Time to run his eyes around the room, time to sneer inwardly at the gaudiness of the place. There's comfort in doing this. Ulyanov and Yanofsky greet him as warmly as before, there is wine as before, there are jokes as before but something is off, there's a pressure in the air.

They speak of the news from Russia. Yanofsky and Ulyanov get cables daily and Koba learns that the imperial government has dissolved the Duma and published a new electoral law setting precise limits on the representation of the different elements of society.

'Those holding substantial property get sixty percent of electors, peasants get twenty-two percent, merchants get fifteen percent,' says Ulyanov.

'Leaving the urban proletariat with three per cent,' says Yanofsky.

Yes, thank you kindly, Koba thinks. My education in Gori may have had its drawbacks, but I can count.

'What about our deputies?' he says. 'We have fifty representatives in the Duma.'

'Fifty-five. All arrested, though I expect they'll be freed soon and sent home.'

'Told to be good and keep quiet on pain of exile,' says Ulyanov. 'Most of them will obey too.'

'And representation from Central Asia?'

'There will be none.'

'None?'

'None at all. Nicholas has decreed that this new Duma must be Russian in spirit, and that non-Russians must never again be able to influence the empire's affairs.'

Non-Russians. People like Koba.

'It wipes out any gains we've made since the uprisings in 1905,' says Ulyanov.

'Means he has signed his death warrant,' says Koba. 'Means there will be opportunities for us.'

'Agreed. Though it will be some time before we can act on them,' says Yanofsky.

Ulyanov, as ever, has the last word. 'The coup shows the uselessness of the parliamentary approach. We have much serious work to do now this little London sojourn is over.'

The three of them lapse into silence. Expectancy rises off

Yanofsky and Ulyanov like steam off a horse on a cold day. You can smell it. Koba has time to register just how airless the room is. Ulyanov and Yanofsky haven't opened the windows since they arrived in London and now it is fetid with their stale smoke and stale talk. The thick air of circular discussion and political theory. The reek of conspiracy, ambition and paranoia.

He can't put it off any longer.

'I have news about the informers in the party,' says Koba.

'Oh yes?' says Ulyanov. 'And is this news bad, by any chance? I fear it must be.'

He takes a sip from his wine. His voice is mild, his manner urbane. There's something false about it too. It's as if he is playing a role, one that contains lines he finds humorous.

Koba can see what's happening here. Ulyanov thinks he knows what he's about to say. He can tell from the jaunty waggle of his chin. From the gleam in his pouchy eyes, he can see that Yanofsky thinks so, too.

A trap is opening up before Koba.

He is a deer in a forest, hunters all around listening for the crack of a dry twig under his hooves. Waiting for him to dash into the open so they can shoot. These hunters are cheerful too. They know they have their quarry cornered and are already anticipating dipping their hands in his blood.

Koba needs more time to think, to work out a safe passage away. Obvious now that the mission was a trap. Of course he was the target here. How did he not realise?

Ulyanov says, 'You know, sometimes I wonder if even the worst treachery matters all that much.' He blinks, sips at his wine. He has a studiedly distracted air. 'I mean, there are a lot of almost indecently loyal comrades who, despite their commitment, do nothing for the movement, whose ineffi- ciency does actual damage in fact, and there are traitors who are among our most useful workers. Maybe the test shouldn't be loyalty, maybe it should simply be effectiveness.'

'An interesting point,' says Yanofsky. 'What do you think Koba?'

Do they think he'll just offer himself up? That he'll just tell them that he's been furnishing the Okhrana with incriminating material for years but hopes they can overlook it because of the hours he's put in as an organiser, as an administrator, as colonel-in-chief of an irregular band of thieves and cut-throats. Do they really think he'd offer himself up like that? That he'd trust to the mercy of men he knows have ordered scores of killings?

This is the thing with the bourgeoisie. Left-wing or right-wing, they think the proletarians are stupid. They think they'll fall for anything. It's a prejudice that is embedded in them.

'I think anyone whose treason is proved should be shot like a rabid dog. And I think anyone who endangers the work of the party through laziness, disorganisation, personal ambition or poor judgement should also face the highest penalty,' Koba says.

'You'd shoot the slipshod workers along with the actual traitors?'

'You know I would.'

Ulyanov and Yanofsky exchange a look.

'Your uncompromising approach does you credit,' says Ulyanov, drily. 'Anyway, you said you had news.'

Koba notes how both the other men seem to be leaning forward slightly now. Braced like sprinters before the firing of the starting pistol. They think they have him. He takes a breath. There's dust in his mouth. This hotel might be expensive, but it is as dirty and as unhealthy as everything else in this city.

'Is there more wine, Comrade Ulyanov?'

Ulyanov pours. It is thick and treacly stuff. Koba sees himself as if from a distance, as if this was theatre. Sees himself hold the glass up to the light, turning the stem slowly, prolonging the moment where the eyes of the audience are on him. Building the tension. Could he throw himself on their mercy after all? Could he, even now, drink this wine and begin: *Actually, Comrades, there is something I should tell you … something I need to confess …*

Koba looks above his shoulder at one of the paintings of haughty, sorrowful women. Young, beautiful and rich, still they have the look of prisoners, of people sentenced to long terms of confinement with no prospect of parole.

He must break cover now. He takes a deep draught of the wine. He clears his throat.

'If you search Maxim Litvinov's quarters in Tower House you will find certain incriminating material.'

He stops there. Ulyanov's face is a mask. Yanofsky huffs and puffs, wriggles on his seat, pulls at his mad hair. He is obviously stricken by this news. Too obviously stricken. A clown, thinks Koba. A clown and a bad actor. Who would be fooled by this pantomime?

But knowing who the hunters are, knowing the weapons they have, knowing that half of them are cack-handed fools, none of this necessarily helps the hunted. If you are trapped you are trapped, if you are outnumbered you are outnumbered. A good Socialist acknowledges the facts. Faces things as they are, not how they wish them to be. Works out a plan that deals with hard realities.

'What kind of incriminating material?'

Ulyanov's chair sighs as he leans back and sips at his drink. He yawns. Economical, quick. Mouth opening and closing neatly. He moistens his lips with his tongue. As Yanofsky is too agitated, so Ulyanov is too calm.

If she were here, Maria Andreyeva would have things to say about the dubious plausibility of the acting.

Koba keeps his eyes on Ulyanov's face. His smooth skin, his neat beard, his calculating eyes. Koba keeps his voice crisp, matter of fact. 'Letters to our enemies, a list of other people working for the Okhrana clearly intended to help the security apparatus of the British state, plus plans for the Tiflis expropriation.' He pauses, sees, just for a second, something flare in Ulyanov's eyes. Excitement, exhilaration, something very close to joy.

Suddenly the correct path opens up. It always does.

Koba has no faith in God and puts no trust in other men, but he has a belief that at the perfect moment the correct words, the right actions will arrive. Sometimes he believes it is possible to move yourself into the space where a God could be.

He allows himself a smile. Takes a swallow of this syrupy wine. Runs a hand through his thick, dark hair. Straightens his back. Gazes at Ulyanov steadily.

'It is, of course, evidence that must be disregarded.'

The hungry light in Ulyanov's eyes fades slightly.

Koba continues, 'It is – obviously – material planted to discredit Litvinov, an effort to ensure his removal from the Bolshevik leadership. It is, in fact, a compliment to Comrade Litvinov. A testament to his effectiveness.'

Yanofsky coughs. Is there such a thing as a disappointed cough? The tension in the air slackens.

'And how do you know this?' Ulyanov runs a hand over his bald dome. He is frowning, irritated.

Koba shrugs. 'The young lad who runs things at Tower House told me he was asked to construct a hiding place in Maxim's trunk and place the items in it. I believe a way would have been found to let me, or someone else in the leadership, know where it was. A crude plot and one I like to think that we would never have fallen for.' He can feel his heart pulsing, feel the blood moving in his veins. There's the sour taste in his mouth, that often comes before some necessary violence. 'I have to say that I am not impressed, Comrade Ulyanov.'

'What?' Ulyanov's mouth turns down, his eyes hooded.

'When you asked me to discover who the traitor was within the ranks of the party, it was an obvious ruse to test my own loyalty. To see what I would do. You already know that Comrade Litvinov is above reproach, but it seems you were less sure about me. You wanted to see if I would seek to discredit him and in doing so reveal my own perfidy. A cheap trick.'

To Ulyanov's credit he doesn't bother to deny it. 'Well, you were seen with known spies several times. In Stockholm and here in London.'

'The Bunins? Rosa Luxemburg and Leo spend every night sharing crackers and gossip with those characters in their hotel. We all associate with spies. It is a distasteful but necessary part of our work. I could hardly have begun to look for unknown informers without contact with the known ones.'

He tells them that of course the Bunins tried to recruit him. Seduction is their job – a job they do badly by the way – and yes, the party line is to ignore scum like them when they approach, or to send them away with a choice remark, but is this the best option?

'When your enemy tugs at your sleeve, it makes sense to stop and hear what he has to say. You learn more from listening to your opponents than you do by talking to your friends. Even incompetent enemies can teach you something,' he says.

What Koba says is true, in a way. They do, all of them,

associate with known agents of the Tsar. It's hard not to. Ulyanov and Yanofsky could both think of times – at a demonstration, on the way to a supposedly clandestine meeting, in a police cell – when someone, usually a stranger but not always, has suggested that the Tsar's secret police was looking for recruits and that they were just the kind of man they needed. As Koba says the approved response to these approaches is to ignore them. Even if you are in a cell you are expected to just keep quiet until they give up and go away. They usually do go away.

But, thinking about it now, maybe there is something in Koba's strategy, maybe they should see what is in their opponent's hand before they slap it away.

'Every time we speak to our enemies, they give us something that might be useful to us,' says Koba. 'Rosa and Leo know this.'

There is a pause.

'And maybe you will give away something of use to them. Risky tactics, my friend,' Yanofsky says.

Koba shrugs, 'Risky or not. It's how I know for sure that Maxim Litvinov is not an agent.' A meaningful pause. 'My friend.'

'It's not just that it's a risky strategy, it's an unauthorised strategy.'

So pompous. It comes to Koba that he has never liked Yanofsky. When he's in a position of real power he will do something about him. Will clip his nuts for him.

'Yes, and of course authorisation is everything. Look, the Tsar and his lackeys have spies everywhere, they probably know everything about us already. You think our elaborate handshakes and passwords keep our information private? Think again. They already know our hat sizes, shoe sizes, the length of our cocks. But we don't have their resources, we don't have their opportunities to get close to our adversaries.'

Which is when Litvinov steps out to join them from where he has been waiting in the dressing room.

Koba's face is blank, neutral. He is carefully unsurprised. Blithely unastonished.

'Do we really need to know the size of an Okhrana cock?' Litvinov says. 'I already feel sure that it's a small, miserable and unloved thing, mostly unemployed.'

Litvinov is cheerful, his movements loose. He seems almost to pirouette as he moves through the room's musty air to an over-stuffed chaise longue. *Look at us, all friends, drinking wine, having fun even in the midst of difficult moments.* All of this can be intimated in the wriggle of his broad shoulders, in the light of his easy smile, in his bright and dancing eyes.

'We need to know everything, brother,' Koba says. He keeps his voice steady.

Litvinov grins. 'Don't let your feelings be hurt, Comrade Jughashvili. You can't blame the party for conducting a thorough audit of its own leadership from time to time.'

'Comrade Litvinov did tell us we were wasting our time,' says Yanofsky.

'But what about the list of names of other agents? Thirteen of them, do we think they're all innocent, that the Okhrana are trying to frame them too?' says Ulyanov.

Koba thinks that Ulyanov is struggling to keep irritation from his voice. He was looking forward to the scandal of announcing Koba's treachery. Looking forward to the outrage it would cause. Looking forward to shaking his head in well-rehearsed sorrow as he said that it was his sad duty to reveal the worst kind of corruption in the heart of the party.

Koba has robbed him of that pleasure. He needs to be

careful because Ulyanov will be looking to punish the man who took this moment of triumph away from him.

'Well, many of those might be guilty,' Koba says. 'Maybe all of them. People the Okhrana no longer has any use for. Names of real informers intended to make us suspect the innocent ones like our comrade here.' Koba gestures towards Litvinov.

'This is my thinking too,' says Litvinov. 'And that in itself means the exercise has been worth carrying out. Here, would you like to see the original evidence we found in my trunk? It was a skilful job, by the way. Someone knows his business. So rare to find such craftmanship these days.'

Litvinov pours himself a glass of wine.

'That was our friend Stan,' says Koba

'He'll go far, that lad.'

Now Litvinov unfurls himself from the chaise longue, crosses the room in two quick strides and picks up a sheaf of papers from the neat writing desk that Koba had so envied on his first visit to these rooms.

As he passes the typed sheets over to Koba, he says, casually, 'I was surprised to see the delegate from Tampere on the list of known informants. The feisty Miss Vuokko.'

Koba says nothing, shows no surprise, no interest even.

Litvinov is smiling again. He holds up the list of supposed informers.

'Maybe this gang of disciples will be like Jesus's in reverse. You know, there he had twelve loyal comrades and one Judas, whereas here maybe we have twelve Judases and one saint. It's possible.'

'We can't waste time trying to find saints,' says Koba.

They speak of other things. Should the robbery in Tiflis go ahead now we think the Okhrana know all about it? They talk about it for some time but in the end they decide yes, let's just change the day. Maybe hit another bank in a different city first in a kind of feint.

Koba says well then, they'll need more men, more ammunition.

It is time for him to go but Ulyanov has one more thing to say.

'Koba, my old friend, should you wish to be present at the interrogation of Miss Vuokko, she's being held here.' He hands over a piece of notepaper on which is scrawled an address. 'I understand that you might have advice for our investigators, that you have useful expertise in this area. Mikhail Tskhakaya is leading the Court of Honour.'

'Tskhakaya? Really? Is he the man for this kind of work?'

'He seemed keen to do it. Very keen. I indulged him. A kind of reward for his loyal service.'

As Koba leaves the house, as he steps into the warm afternoon, he closes his eyes and concentrates for a moment on the warm sun on his face. A moment of reprieve. He knows that he is expected to hurry over to where Elli Vuokko is being held. It's another test. Or, if it isn't, it will probably do no harm to treat it as if it was one. He should be there to question her, to help decide whether to despatch her or to secure her freedom, and judgements will be made about him based on his choices.

There is, however, also value in showing indifference to her fate. In any case, with Tskhakaya in charge nothing will be done quickly, and this is good because there is something else that needs attending to first. Koba needs to see a boy about a bullfinch.

22

Dignity

Mikhail Tskhakaya – Barsov, the Leopard – is forty-two and has already been a revolutionary communist for twenty-seven years. As a young man he helped found and run the study groups for industrial workers in Georgia. He is a teacher, a thinker and a windbag. If party members in Tiflis upset the local leadership, they are sometimes sentenced to attend his lectures on Marxist theory.

He reminds Elli of the Lutheran preachers of her childhood. She listens to him talk and she knows she should be scared, but she is so thoroughly taken back to the long dreary Sunday school mornings – a perpetual grey-pink half-light glowing through small windows into austere square rooms with their hard benches – that she is merely sleepy. She's also reassured. She knows it's not logical. Dull people can be more dangerous than livelier ones when given power but it's hard to stay at a high pitch of nervousness when someone is boring the arse off you.

They had picked her up just after she had seen Rosa on to the train. It was disappearing in a roiling cloud of dark, choking smoke and Elli had turned to find her exit from the platform barred by an impassive woman from Minsk and a nervy little man from Tomsk. They had been polite as they invited her into their hackney cab but it was clear there was to be no argument, no debate. She would go with them and she would do what she was told.

She had asked where she was going and on whose orders was she going there? What was she supposed to have done, and, whatever it was, who had accused her of doing it? She didn't get any answers and she hadn't expected any. The blank-faced lady from Minsk said it would be best if she saved her energy. Elli looked at her more closely as they travelled. She was pretty sure she recognised her from the early morning workouts.

'I'll miss them, won't you?' she said.

Minsk was confused. 'What?'

'Mrs Garrud's training sessions.'

The woman relaxed a little, smiled, 'Yes, yes I will. Good fun. I'm going to keep it up when I get home.'

'Pain is only weakness leaving the body,' said Elli. 'I will also keep training when I get home.'

The woman had looked away, glanced out of the window. And it was clear to Elli what this meant: *she doesn't expect me to get home.* She had been scared then, icy fingers reaching into her belly. However, an hour sitting in the mildewed parlour of a backstreet terrace had eroded the fear until it became a kind of deadened stupefaction, and the few minutes of barely comprehensible interrogation that followed has done nothing to sharpen her feelings.

She yawns and sees Tskhakaya flinch. She apologises and wonders if the yawn could be what condemns her to execution. Women have to assume that all men are touchy, easily offended. Dangerous when slighted. *Even I know you don't laugh at men.* Clearly you don't yawn at them either.

This is when she remembers Tskhakaya's nickname. It doesn't suit him. She wonders if he gave it to himself.

'I'm sorry,' she says. 'Last night in London. It was a late

one. You know how it is.' She gives him the full beam of her smile.

Tskhakaya frowns and she suspects that he has never been impulsive or reckless or allowed himself to become uncontrolled. Has never known how it is.

Elli Vuokko understands that she is being held on suspicion of some kind of treason. That she might have spilled secrets. That she might be in the pay of the Tsar, that she has been denounced in some mysterious way. There's a letter. A list. It is all nonsensical, and the hesitant digressive way that Tskhakaya runs the interview makes it all seem like the stuff of an oppressive dream.

It is time to get a little clarity, to get some control of the situation.

'Comrade Tskhakaya, Mikhail, please tell me plainly what exactly have I done?'

'You know what you've done.'

'I don't and I'm beginning to think you don't either.'

'Insolence won't help.'

She very nearly laughs. Catches herself in time, turns it into a cough.

'Are you ill?' He sounds solicitous, genuinely concerned. He sniffs. Fact is, thinks Elli, that it is her interrogator that doesn't look well. There's a sheen of sweat across his forehead, his hands shake.

'Honestly, it's just a hangover,' she says.

Nina Kropin had insisted that they share a bottle of wine. After that it had seemed bad manners for Elli not to get a second and after that they had pooled their remaining English money to get a third, alternately giggling and shushing each other. It wasn't explicitly forbidden to drink on the premises of Langton House, but the whole feel of the place was pro-temperance. Sobriety was embedded in the very stones. The sense of breaking taboos was every bit as intoxicating as the rough red wine.

Tskhakaya sighs. The sigh is eloquent and speaks with more precision than anything he has so far articulated with actual words. *I just don't understand young women today* it says. The plaintive message that is eventually uttered by every middle-aged man.

Elli has to cough again.

He takes a step forward towards her. She smiles at him. Opens her mouth to apologise for the cough. He smacks her hard across the face.

Tears spring to her eyes. Her chest is tight. The metal taste of blood in her mouth. She puts her hand to her cheek, blinks up at Tskhakaya. He looks benign, an avuncular teacher.

'I hope you will now give me your full attention.' He is smiling.

Three empty hours going around and around the same dead ground. He doesn't slap her again, but the threat of calmly brutal violence has seeped into the air of the room. She keeps her eyes on the uneven flags of the floor and when she's asked a question she keeps her voice quiet and her tone respectful. She repeats – over and over – that there has been some mistake, some mix-up, but it is clear that her thoughts on the matter are not really necessary in order for this court to do its work.

At last the investigation – the trial – seems to be over. At least, the Leopard eventually stops growling and pacing. Tskhakaya, plainly judge as well as investigating officer and prosecuting counsel, now has to decide the sentence.

Elli knows that he is enjoying all these roles very much. Knows too that having her in his power gives him pleasure as a man and not simply as a party officer. She understands that he will take his time. She knows too that the evidence he considers will only partly be denunciations and whether her name is on any list of party infiltrators. What will weigh most heavily will be her attitude, whether she has seemed impressed enough by her interrogator's manner and intellect. Whether she has seemed sufficiently frightened of him. Whether it gives him more pleasure to give life or to take it.

She knows she should fear the worst.

Two unsmiling, bored-looking men – brainless thugs, *roistot* – take her to the cellar of the house where she is made to sit on a metal trunk. Her hands are tied in front of her, her feet bound together. The object of the tying up is not so much to prevent escape as to humiliate. She understands this. What she can't understand is why she still doesn't feel more scared. She should be terrified, hysterical. Instead she is calm.

So this is how her life ends, before it really gets started. A shame, but millions die in unfair ways every day. They die of sickness, of cold, of hunger, in accidents and in wars. They die of over-work and for lack of simple medicines. They die of broken hearts and shattered spirits. And they die because someone they barely know decides that they must for reasons that no one understands. What's one more senseless death more or less?

It's her youth that enables her to be this fatalistic. An older person, knowing how precious and fleeting life is, would be shouting, cursing, pleading. And none of it would help.

The room is dark and damp. It smells strongly of river water and decaying paper. The bare flagstones of the cellar have a wet gleam and here and there are tea chests full of buff-coloured files of the kind used by civil servants. There are boxes of old books too. Random titles in a variety of languages, nothing she recognises. If she had to guess she'd say they seem to be saucy French romances, English adventure stories, Russian poetry. A child's arithmetic primer.

She sits in the dark, passing the time by thinking about everybody she has ever met. Trying to recall all their names. It's a thing she does sometimes, usually on those nights when sleep is slow to arrive.

She is up to the people she met in her last term at her elementary school when there is a disturbance by the stairs and a blindfolded man is brought in and forced down onto the floor on the other side of the room, where he twitches and squirms.

He makes the desperate bleat of a frightened lamb in the slaughterhouse shed. Like Elli he has hands and legs tied and he has a telltale wetness between his legs that shows Elli that he is panicked by what is about to happen.

Elli closes her eyes. Senses heightened, she can hear the man's shallow breaths, the chuckle of the nearby river and behind that noise a scuttling that suggests mice or rats. Still her own fear refuses to arrive. She is fairly sure she won't piss herself any time soon but there is anger, frustration. If she gets the chance she will punch someone before she goes. She relaxes into imagining her fist catching Tskhakaya right in the solar plexus, the choked gasp as he doubles up, the crack as she follows the first hit, cuffing his head hard enough to send him to the ground. Maybe she'd have a chance to get a couple of kicks in before the roistot drag her away.

'Who is that? Who's there?' The Russian from across the room is high-pitched and querulous, but defiant too. 'Come on then, finish what you started.'

Elli opens her eyes, the man is twisting, struggling against the ropes that bind him.

'Hey, calm down,' she says. 'You need some dignity.'

'Do I? Is it dignity I need?' The man barks out a short laugh. He struggles to a sitting position. 'And they've sent a woman to do the job have they? No fucking dignity in that. I might not have dignity lady, but your lot, you have no fucking shame.'

After this sudden blaze of anger, the man slumps back onto the floor.

'Hush,' Elli says. 'I'm not here to question you or to ... or to do anything else. I'm a prisoner here too. We're in the same boat.'

After a few seconds the man sits upright again, 'A fucking boat?' he laughs, a dry bark, that makes her aware of the inanity of her remark. 'Excuse my language, love, but I'm under some stress.'

'You're excused. I'm not easily shocked.'

They lapse into silence again. The man's breathing seems easier and Elli finds she's pleased to have been of some use. She closes her eyes again, listens again to the sounds of water, to that pitter-pat of animal feet skittering among the boxes and debris of the room. She tries to return to thinking of her list of all the people she's met in her life.

'So,' the man's voice startles her. 'What did you do?'

'Me?'

'Unless there's any other people here. I mean, there could be. I'm bloody blindfolded after all.'

'There's no one else here. And I did nothing.'

'Really? Innocent, eh?'

'Yes.'

'Come on, love, don't give me that.'

She stays quiet.

'Well, I can tell you something for nothing. I'm guilty. I did it. I did it all.'

'What did you do?'

'Everything they said.'

'And what was that?'

The man seems to have to make an effort to remember.

'Gave the authorities names and dates, places where weapons are stored. Drew pictures of enemies of the state. Took photographs even. Copied map references. Did it all. I'd do it again too. I'm not ashamed. I did it to save my country. To save Russia. They should give me a fucking medal. They should make a statue of me, put it up in the main square in Uglich.'

'You're from Uglich?'

'Yes. A lovely place. Sad that I won't see it again. And what about you? You're not Russian.'

'I'm from Finland.'

'Beautiful people, the Finns.'

'Some are.'

They lapse into silence again. When he speaks next his voice is quieter, she doesn't catch what he says at first. 'What?'

'I said I wonder which of us they will shoot first.'

'Well,' she says, 'I hope it's you.'

'What?' He sounds shocked, hurt. 'Why?'

'So I can die knowing that I've seen a cancer properly cut out. Seen a traitor destroyed.'

'Even though you'll be next?'

'For treachery, for sending good comrades to their death, it's better that a hundred innocent people are killed than one guilty person escape.'

'You don't believe that.'

'I do.' Does she? It's what she used to believe, but she isn't sure any more.

'I guess it's true what they say about Finnish women.'

'What?'

'That they are beautiful but also cold. Hard.'

'Only when we need to be.'

'Sounds like you'd shoot me yourself.'

'Of course I would. In a moment. At least then I could be sure I'd done some good for the people before I leave this world. And I'm a good shot. I wouldn't miss. I'd do it clean.'

They fall quiet again. She finds she can't leave it like that.

'Tell me about Uglich. Tell me what there is to see there.'

So he does. He tells her about the historic Russian architecture, about the Alexeievsky and Resurrection monasteries, about the Assumption three-tented church, about the beautiful countryside, friendliness of the people, the food.

He speaks fluently and without pause for at least ten minutes before he falls quiet.

'Sounds lovely.'

'The best place in Russia for a boy to grow up.'

There is pride in his voice, though to be honest it sounds like just another unimportant place spawning unimportant lives. Just another ordinary Russian town.

Shortly after that, the roistot come for the man. They say nothing as they untie his legs and hands and remove the blindfold. He doesn't speak to them and he doesn't resist. Goes meekly, walking unsteadily, supported by his guards.

As he passes Elli he nods, gives a wan smile, holds out a hand. She notices how it trembles. She raises her own tied hands to take it. His fingers are thin, his skin hot. She is misted in the smell of his urine. She keeps her face blank, doesn't show any distaste.

'Despite everything, I'm glad to have met you, Miss. You made a dark time a little brighter. Thank you.'

His eyes glisten.

'You are one of the beautiful Finns,' he says.

She turns her face away and tries not to hear the man's stumbling steps up the cellar staircase.

23

A Beautiful Fellow

Koba scribbles a few words on a piece of writing paper torn from the pad on which he has been composing his letters to Kato. Not that he has sent any after that first one. He folds it, writes an address in English on it.

'Can you take this? It is to be given only to the person it is addressed to.'

'It's quite a schlepp. A long walk, I mean,' says Arthur.

'Take this,' Koba holds out two shiny half-crowns. Five shillings for a couple of miles walk. Good money for a simple job. Generous even by Koba's standards. 'Make sure you give the note to no one else. And before you go, please bring me the object I left outside.'

'The thing in the hall?'

'The thing in the hall, yes.'

Thomas Bacon decides it is time to assert himself, to get his voice in the room. 'You can't give my son orders,'

'It's okay Da.'

The man subsides into mutinous silence.

In the hallway is a large birdcage with a heavy woollen blanket over it. It's quite a struggle for Arthur to bring it into the kitchen. He sets it down and stands back to look at it with curiosity. It is quite clear he is itching to whip that blanket away.

'Time to go, Arthur,' says Koba.

Arthur glances at his father. Thomas scowls and looks away. Says nothing. Shy, his son nudges him. Thomas sees that the boy is holding out the coins that Koba gave him a moment ago. He waits a moment, gives his son a look of contempt, before he takes and pockets the money.

Arthur looks towards Koba, raises his hand and leaves the kitchen. Thin fingers, beautifully shaped. Musicians' fingers. Artists' fingers. Fingers you can't imagine ever forming a fist.

When Koba hears Arthur slam the door behind him he takes the blanket off the cage, and reveals that it is occupied by a tiny bird. A song begins immediately. A cascade of notes signalling confusion, alarm and distress. The same emotions that Koba sees now on the face of the pugnacious man across the room from him.

'What's this?' says Thomas Bacon. His voice is dangerously soft. Perhaps he has some real fight in him after all.

'This is a bird,' Koba says. 'A singing bird. But as you know this kind only learn one song so you and your son should choose carefully before teaching it.'

'I don't want a fucking bird. I'll wring its fucking neck.'

'No. Mr Bacon. Sir. You won't do that. Nothing must happen to this bird. If it dies, it must be because it gets too old. No other reason can be allowed. I'm told these birds live for five years if they are treated well, so if I find this one has died before 1912, I will be upset. Very upset. He is beautiful fellow, no?'

He is. Salmon pink breast, grey back, black cap and tail, and bright white rump. It is like an imperial army uniform. The sort of thing the Tsar might make his household soldiers wear. Koba can imagine it. Tall guardsmen in grey coats with pink facings, white jackets, black hats, white trousers. Yes, Tsar Nicholas would love an army dressed like that.

The bird's rump flashes as he hops, agitated, from perch to floor of the cage and back. He has already been shitting everywhere. Those who are trapped and scared foul their own spaces before they get desperate enough to try for freedom.

'And if he should die – or escape – I will expect you to purchase another and make sure you teach him the same song.'

In slow, deliberate English, every word delivered as though it were a heavy weight, he tells Thomas Bacon a story. He tells him about what they did to a famous enemy of socialism in the city of Ozersk. How they killed him quickly and efficiently, kindly almost, but then went on to kill – less efficiently, less kindly – the man's wife, his brother, his sister, his mother, his wife's mother and, of course, his baby son. It was hard but necessary. They needed to send a message. And what was the man's crime? He showed a reckless, ultimately fatal, lack of respect. A truly despicable absence of fear. He had persistently, and despite being asked to desist, made fun of Socialist leaders in the city where he lived. He had mocked their accents, their manners, the way they walked, their taste in women. He had implied that they were gangsters, extortionists, hoodlums and not even competent ones. He had showed extremely poor judgement and eventually he – and his family and friends – had paid the price.

The party didn't regret it, either. It was now very strong in Ozersk. Party leaders treated with proper deference. You could say it was a hotbed of revolutionary activity.

'We said to you before that you should not believe what is in the capitalist press. And you shouldn't. We are much more dangerous than they think. Much more brutal too.'

'All these threats over a fucking bird? I don't get it.'

'If I am so serious about the life of a pet, how much more serious will I be about any harm that comes to my friend Arthur. Your son.'

Koba sees that the man gets it now. Sees his face change, the purple heat rise in it.

'I'll bring up my bloody son in any damn way—'

Koba raises his hand. Thomas stops mid-sentence.

'I have another story.'

He tells his landlord of a rainy February night in Tevali, the capital of Kakhetia in Eastern Georgia. A man in middle age staggering from a local *dukhan*, one of the wine cellars where drunkards, vagrants and petty criminals gather. This man is called Vissarion. Another man follows him. This second man is younger, in his late twenties perhaps. A man wearing a distinctive quilted jacket, a man who stalks the older drunk to a deserted street where he pulls an axe from inside his jacket and strikes Vissarion hard on the head, once, twice, three times, before finishing off his unconscious victim with multiple knife thrusts to the body. So much blood. Amazing to think that one shrunken, drink-ravaged body would have so much blood in it.

And what was the younger man's motive? It wasn't robbery. The victim had nothing worth taking.

The local police didn't waste much time on the case. For them it was just another ne'er-do-well dying in a simple drunken brawl. The truth though was that this was not a fight, nor was it a murder. This was justice. Vengeance for crimes that had taken place many years earlier. Crimes committed against a child.

In his stumbling English, Koba finds a way to tell Thomas Bacon that children grow up and the memories of their grievances grow with them, and sometimes those children take those grievances and travel with them to where the man who inflicted that grief lives. Sometimes they put on their favourite quilted jacket and they carry out the sentence decided upon many years before in the heart of a boy.

There is a silence then, a quiet moment, where Koba sees that Thomas Bacon has taken in what he is wearing. A quilted jacket, one that has clearly seen better days.

Koba smiles, strokes his moustache. Scratches at his pitted cheeks.

'If I hear that Arthur is hurt. Or sad even, then ...' Koba finds he has run out of words and so makes a graphic cutting gesture with a finger across his throat. A universal sign understood by everyone, even dense Englishmen like Thomas Bacon. The Englishman blinks rapidly.

Koba smiles cheerfully. 'You know I will do this. I did it to my own father, and I took pleasure in it.' He claps his hands. 'And I will take pleasure in doing it to you.'

24

Gratitude

Despite her fantasies of resistance, Elli goes quietly when they come. She aches. Everything hurts. She spends some moments after being untied rubbing her arms and legs, to coax the blood back into hands and feet. How long has she been sitting on that metal trunk? Two hours? Three?

Up the cellar stairs, twitching away from the hands of her jailers, through a filthy kitchen, a massacre of dirty plates and mugs, down a narrow hallway trying not to touch the brown, slimy walls, and into the drab parlour. Everything in it so mean and small and beige. She feels so tired now, and impatient with the way things are. It's as if she has become suddenly old. Let's just get it done.

The Leopard seems to have grown into his name during the hours where Elli Vuokko was in the cellar. Seems more robust. He has the goons push her to her knees while he prowls the room, shoulders back, head high, growling out his lecture on the sacrifices involved in being in a leadership position in a revolutionary organisation, the need to put aside personal considerations, or even ordinary human emotions such as tenderness. She keeps her eyes on the filthy parlour floor, all crumbs and mysterious smears, dots of lard, jam, and substances that don't bear inspection. Specks of what might be blood too.

She can't listen to what her judge-executioner is saying. She knows already that begging and pleading won't help, will just give him extra gratification. If she was to speak it would be to ask really, Tskhakaya all this because you were too shy to make a pass at me? Because you were too clumsy to woo me properly? Because I wouldn't talk to you in the Rose Street Club? Because I wouldn't walk with you listening to your lists of facts, sighing with admiration? Because you're jealous of the real men of action, men who know how to ask for what they want?

For a moment she mourns the possible lives she's losing. The men she won't sleep with, the babies she won't have, the liberation she won't be able to fight for, the freedoms she won't help bring into being. The new world that she won't ever live to see.

As Tskhakaya growls on, his voice as monotonous as the turning of the lathes back in Tampere, she entertains herself with outrageous fantasies of rescue. She remembers her determination to take a chance to grab at Tskhakaya's legs if he comes close, a scenario where she topples him and gets a few digs in before the roistot drag her away – she is still fully committed to that plan – but now she also imagines a scene where Edith Garrud leads Rosa Luxemburg and a force of revolutionary women into this squalid little house, drop-kicking the guards and chopping the Leopard down, reversing their roles so that Tskhakaya is on his knees begging for his life, while Elli strokes her chin and delivers self-aggrandising homilies. They would be shouting as they transfer the pain from their own bodies into those of her jailors. Hell, maybe they'd be singing.

The idea makes her laugh. Tskhakaya stops mid-peroration, astonished. He's never seen such blatant disregard for the rituals of a Court of Honour.

What happens next is perhaps just as surprising as the arrival of a crack squad of female commandos.

The next words Elli hears are not from an outraged Tskhakaya, but instead are delivered in the soft dry, polite, faintly amused tones of the leading Menshevik.

Martov! Martov, accompanied by Plekhanov, both of them sleek and prosperous and thoroughly out of place here as they ask the Leopard if they might have a quick word outside.

A minute later – it really was a quick word – the men are back in the room. Tskhakaya gestures for her to rise. After so much time kneeling awkwardly it is a struggle. Martov extends a hand to help. His skin is as soft and dry as his voice.

'Congratulations, my dear,' says Martov, smiling.

'Yes, congratulations, my dear,' says Plekhanov. He is also smiling and Elli remembers that Comrade Plekhanov is famous for never having an original thought of his own, never making a remark anyone will remember more than ten minutes after he's uttered it. She tries hard to recall his opening speech to the Congress but beyond a vague sense that it was a standard call for compromise nothing comes back to her.

'After a thorough investigation, conducted with, ah, exemplary efficiency by Comrade Tskhakaya, nothing has been found against you and you are free to go, to return to Tampere and to continue your work there.' Martov's smile broadens. He has expensive teeth. Elli thinks for a moment that he might be about to suggest a hug.

'Yes, you are free to return to Tampere,' says Plekhanov.

A bottle of vodka appears from somewhere. Plekhanov pours, toasts are drunk. Martov talks. Plekhanov repeats what he says. Tskhakaya says nothing. He makes sure that he is always looking away from her, that there is no danger she will ever catch his eye.

There's a wild moment when Elli thinks about asking after the man that was held in the cellar with her. The man from Uglich. But it is a moment that soon passes.

Instead Elli simply nods and smiles at everything that is said. Yes, it is shocking about Stolypin's coup, yes it gives fresh impetus to the formation of broad alliances against the regime, yes much has been accomplished at this Congress. There are unspoken agreements too, the implicit answers to the questions Martov and Plekhanov don't ask but which hover in the room regardless. Yes, I'm grateful you have come here to rescue me. Yes, you are like knights of old. Like saints, almost. So, yes, I owe you my gratitude. Yes, you can count on me in the future if you need to. Yes, yes, yes to everything.

After three rounds of drinks, she asks to be excused and is shown to a stinking lavatory across a cobbled yard. She takes her time getting there. Pausing to look at the glutinous clouds moving heavily across the sky, to feel the tired breeze on her face, to notice how the viciously yellow dandelions push their way through the cracks between the stones, the pink roses that manage to fight for a space amid the nettles in the corner of the neglected plot. There's a haze in the air, the vague smell of cooked meat. The breath catches in her throat. She coughs.

She notices the upturned metal bucket, blackened as if burned recently, crows tearing at the body of a skinny rat, traces of gore on the ground. They are bold, these birds. They don't fly off but continue their meal ignoring Elli. There are thick smears of blood on the cobbles. The yard has been used to slaughter something recently. Beyond the wooden fence that surrounds the space, she can hear children shouting, a donkey braying. The vodka burns in her belly.

She doesn't return to the house after using the toilet. Instead, she pushes open the gate to the yard, winces as the hinges complain. She expects one of the guards to appear and force her back into the room with the revolution's dullest men. Her face aches with all the smiling she's done, with all the thankfulness she's had to show.

Why do women always have to express gratitude for things that should be basic? Things like being listened to. Things like not being murdered.

25

Something With a Bit of Oomph

In Jubilee Street they are worried about Tskhakaya. He came home from presiding over the Court of Honour flushed and hot. Collapsed into a chair like a man of eighty-two rather than forty-two. Talking but making no sense. Gasping for painful breaths. Temperature of thirty-nine.

Koba and Thomas Bacon had to help him up the stairs and into bed. Now, it is morning and he seems worse.

Out on the landing they hold a little medical conference.

'*Gripi*,' says Koba. Influenza.

'Well, he can't stay here.'

'And he can't move from here.'

'You've only paid until tonight and I need the room.'

'We can pay. I think we'll need at least three more days.'

'What if he dies? I don't want him dying.'

'He won't die.'

Yet, when Koba pops his head back into the bedroom, when he looks at Tskhakaya's ashen face, when he sees the panic in his glittering eyes, when he hears the strangled wheeze of his attempts to get enough air, he feels he might be being optimistic. In Georgia gripi is often deadly.

'He won't die,' Koba says again, even more emphatically this time.

'Still, I don't want him here.'

Koba turns his gaze on Thomas Bacon. The man looks

away. Pathetic. Feeble. Koba waits a long moment, then turns and walks downstairs to the kitchen, where a fretful Arthur paces. Thomas follows, huffing.

'Arthur, I leave for Europe soon and I promised you a story. I will tell it to you now if you like.'

'Stories now is it?' says Thomas Bacon in disgust. 'I'm going outside for a smoke, enjoy the sun for a bit.'

'What kind of story is it, Mr Ivanovich? Is it a true one or a made up one?'

'It is both.' He tells the boy that this is the story of something that might happen. That should happen. That will happen if everyone does what they should.

'See this now, Arthur. In your head. See me, your friend Mr Ivanovich. Koba. See me drinking my good qvevri wine in the Tilipuchuri Tavern. See I am happy. See I smile as I look at everything and everyone. You see, Arthur, this is the story of a robbery.'

Koba closes his eyes. In his mind he can see it happening, as clearly as if it were taking place in front of him right now.

'The police will have been warned, that is obvious. There will be gendarmes everywhere, soldiers in the windows of shops. Guns. Lots of guns. Our lads dressed as peasants and standing on street corners, trying to look at home.

Except for Kamo. Kamo will be dressed as a cavalry captain and sitting on a one-horse carriage. One of those fast carriages built for speed and manoeuvrability. A phaeton. He will sit and talk nonsense to his horse as he waits for the action to begin'. Koba looks at Arthur's expectant face, such concentration there.

'At thirty minutes after ten in the morning, lights will flash. The stagecoach is here! The boys leave the tavern, pistols ready. Your friend Ivanovich finishes his drink and follows them. He'll watch things for a minute or two then go to the flop – the meeting place. Into the Square now come the Cossacks. Arthur, they are beautiful. Blue coats, tall hats, their beards, their proud stares. They are as beautiful as their horses, and the horses are magnificent. Lean, black, their sweat shining. Behind them, the stagecoach. Inside the stagecoach, the money. 400,000 roubles sent from Moscow to pay the wages of the bureaucrats who sit on their fat and ever-spreading backsides. With the sacks of money, two bank men and two guards with rifles. Behind the stagecoach another phaeton, this one bigger than Kamo's. Two horses and it is filled with soldiers. These soldiers are not like the Cossacks. Bored children, most of them. Still, they have carbines and maybe they can use them. It is possible.

'Picture this, Arthur. The Square crowded with people. Housewives shopping, men gossiping, people just passing the time. Some have come especially to see soldiers and horses. More lights flash and our boys leave their street corners and hit the carriage with grenades. Boom-Boom-Boom! The noise! Like being kicked in the stomach, the head, the balls. Panic, not just in the Square but across the whole city. Carriages and carts overturned, people running everywhere, in all directions. Children fall under hooves, fall under the wheels of waggons. Bright blood on the cobbles, turning it slippery. All the glass in the square shattered. No more windows. Chimneys falling.

'The boys follow the grenades with shooting. They shoot at the police, at the soldiers in the windows. The Cossacks fight with dying horses. Not beautiful now. Horse guts in their mouths. In their beards. And the screaming. Have you heard a horse scream? Arthur, you don't want to.

One of the horses tied to the bank stagecoach runs. Four of the boys chase it. One throws a grenade – blows its legs off. The coach stops.

'The boys are in and getting the money. The guards do nothing. They shit themselves. Kamo rides up. Fires his pistol in air. Our boys throw sacks into his phaeton. He rides from the square where he meets police! They shoot. They miss. Kamo shouts at them to look at his bloody uniform, can't they see he's a cavalry captain! He has the money. It's safe. Now you police, you need to get in the Square and stop the robbers. The police salute. They apologise. So sorry, Sir. The noise. They run into the Square. Kamo curses them as they go. Imbeciles! Morons! Cretins! Useless fucking bumpkins! Don't waste more time! Get stuck in!

'Arthur, I wish you could be there. Many soldiers and police dead. Forty or more. Fifty! Others injured, whimpering where they fall. None of our boys caught and much money for the party. It will be a good day's work. Of course Martov and his group will sulk like schoolgirls. Whine like bitches. Drone on about how we promised not to do anything like this. How we gave our word after the great favour he did us, but Arthur, Martov and his kind are spineless. Self-indulgent drinkers of warm milk. Masturbators. You can't change the world with people like that. For real action you need people from the street. You need men of stone. Men of steel.' He stops. Smiles down at the boy.

'There. A story as good as those in your precious *Vanguard*?'

'Yes. It was exciting, the way you told it. Maybe it would have been even more exciting if I'd been able to understand it.'

Koba is shocked.

'If you'd told it in English, I mean. You started in English but switched to your own language when you got really into it.'

He'd told the whole thing in Georgian without realising!

'Never mind, though, Mr Ivanovich, it still sounded amazing. I loved the sound of it. Like music.'

Koba laughs. 'What a fool I am, Arthur. Why didn't you tell me?'

'I didn't like to interrupt.'

Oh, this child. So sweet, so polite, so soft, so unsuited to the modern world. He didn't like to interrupt. Koba feels tears welling and he surprises them both by hugging Arthur.

After a moment, he can trust himself to speak, 'And now we should fix our sick friend upstairs some good strong tea. Here, I'll show you how to make it the Georgian way. The proper way.'

It is a few minutes after the telling of the story when Koba is surprised by Elli Vuokko turning up at the door of the house. Behind her stand the ghosts of both his father and Akaki Gotsridze. Seeing the three of them together makes his throat constrict. What does it mean?

He is so relieved when Elli speaks that he punches the air. One thing he knows about the dead, is that they don't speak.

'You're alive!' he says. He almost embraces her. Starts forward but stops himself. His father and Gotsridze have similar sly, grinning expressions. Dead men or not, he wants to reach past the girl and hit them. Bang their heads together.

'Yes, I'm alive,' she says.

She tells him that she wants a quick word with Mikhail Tskhakaya and he tells her that it is impossible. Comrade Tskhakaya is sick. He has had a night so restless that none of them got any sleep. They spent it watching him, fetching him water, soothing his brow. Koba was even holding his hand at one point. He absolutely can't see visitors.

'You're his nurse!' says Elli. She sounds delighted.

'Yes.'

'Being a nurse is not so different from being a revolutionary, I suppose.'

He waits for her to explain. He guesses that she will mention something about both revolutionaries and nurses needing empathy and compassion.

'Both get to bury their mistakes,' she says.

They move down the hall and to the kitchen. The dead men don't follow. Why so shy, he thinks. He almost says it out loud.

He sees her clock the other occupants. The sad-eyed boy, the ham-faced man. She smiles at them, says how pleased she is to see Arthur again and how she is sure he is taller and even more handsome than when she had seen him last. She shakes hands with Thomas Bacon, compliments him on the cleanliness and good order of his kitchen. The man actually blushes as Elli directs her warmth to him, widens her smile. Charm is like a false passport, a document that can take you anywhere. A magic power. A trick.

She is enchanted with the bird. 'Who is this gorgeous creature?'

'This is Archie, my new bullfinch. Mr Ivanovich got him for me.' Arthur smiles shyly at Koba, which means Elli turns curious eyes towards him.

Koba's turn to blush. Curse the boy.

Elli laughs.

The bird flings handfuls of notes at the air.

'A beautiful voice,' Elli says.

'We're going to teach him to sing an actual song,' says Arthur.

'Oh, yes? What?'

'We haven't decided yet. It's a big decision because finches can only learn one song.'

'You should let Mr Ivanovich teach it something. He is a very good singer. I bet you didn't know that, Arthur.'

'I didn't Miss, no.'

'We'll decide what the bird sings thank you Miss,' says Thomas Bacon, folding meaty arms against his chest. 'And it'll be something English, something rousing. Something with a bit of oomph in it.'

26

We Are Nothing

They go out. The day has become still, the air slowed to soft breath. Afternoon sun threatens to force a way through the clouds. Koba sets a fast pace, as if he has an appointment to keep.

As they walk, Elli tells him the story of being picked up by the people she calls by the names of their home towns, Minsk and Tomsk. She tells him about the interrogation, how dull it was, like being kept behind at school. She tells him of her acquittal. The whole tale got through in brief sentences. She keeps it light. Tells it as though it was a sort of childish prank. Teasing by wanton boys. Koba listens, says nothing.

Without discussing it, they enter a small park, a scrubby green oasis in the smoke-grey city. The buildings around looming like soldiers tired of sentry duty. They lean against each other despite their vows to stay upright, ramrod straight. You could almost imagine them yawning. Koba and Elli sit down on a bench and watch a tiny boy try and fail to fly a kite. They watch the pigeons tussle over the remains of old picnics. The park is busy. Other couples have been tempted out by the prospect of a balmy late afternoon. Koba sees that it is the men talking and the women listening, except for those couples where neither party is talking or listening, those couples that lie entangled. Those couples are wrapped around one another, going at each other in a way that doesn't happen in Gori or Tiflis. No one seems concerned about behaving like this in front of the family groups, or the many people who lie sleeping, desperate to catch up on the rest they missed while walking the streets. Carrying the banner as Arthur would say, trying to stay away from the prodding truncheons of the police.

'I don't know why I'm telling you this,' Elli says.

Koba does. She wants his sympathy, obviously, and she wants to know who has denounced her. Wants to know if he's heard anything. Wants to know if she's still suspected.

Koba bends, picks up a stone and throws it at a pigeon. He doesn't like them. These driven and restless scavengers. The pecking dead.

'Look at them,' he says. 'A perfect symbol of the people of London. Grey and fat. Fighting for scraps.'

'But tough too. And fearless in a way,' Elli says. 'You can't get rid of them.'

'Thomas Bacon is a London pigeon,' he says.

'A classic pigeon. Poor Arthur.'

They sit in silence for a while. The boy with the kite begins to whimper. A nearby adult shouts at the kid, yells what does he expect trying to fly a kite when there's no bleeding wind. Koba tries not to look in their direction. Tries and fails, and when he does there is his father. Next to him is Gotsridze. They never met in the real world, but in the shadow world of the murdered, of course they can be friends. Part of a confederacy of the pathetic dead. They both look his way. Baleful and attempting menace.

He almost laughs. Fuck them. He's seen them both off once, he can do it again.

Elli says, 'Why do the English hate their children?'

Koba doesn't answer. Instead he turns and lunges, kisses

her hard on the mouth. His left arm around her shoulders pulls her in close. His right hand is on her breast.

Her mouth stays closed. He can feel the hard barrier of her strong teeth behind her full lips.

She moves her head away, pushes him back gently, hands on both shoulders. She puts her hands on his face. Hugs him. His hand returns to her breast, the other moves to her neck, strokes gently. He tells her what he wants.

She sighs.

'Hey,' she says, at last. 'The moment for all this has passed for us. I'm going home tomorrow and you're going back to Kato and to your baby.'

He keeps his hand on her for a moment more, before he drops it with a long breath. He doesn't tell her that, actually, he's not going back to Kato. Not just yet. There is business in Berlin. Then Tiflis.

'I saved you,' he says. 'Well, Martov and I. They were going to make you disappear. I sent a note to Martov, told him where you were, told him a mistake was about to be made. Told him he could do himself some good, make an important ally for the Mensheviks.'

He knows he sounds plaintive. Like a child wanting help from a grown up. Like the boy with his kite.

Elli doesn't seem to react at all. It's as if she hasn't heard him. Doesn't look at him. Stares out at the families picnicking, the lovers courting, the unemployed workers sleeping. For a few moments he thinks she hasn't heard.

'Explained how he could earn the gratitude of the famous Girl Nihilist at the very least,' Koba says.

'Why did you do that?'

'Wasn't a mistake about to be made? Hasn't Martov earned the support of the Girl Nihilist? Don't we both owe him something now?'

219

She looks at him sharply. 'And how did you know where I was? Who told you I was suspected?'

Koba says nothing.

'In any case, they had no evidence.'

Still Koba says nothing. He doesn't need to. They both know that there are people in the party for whom accusation is proof enough. A pointing finger can be all it takes to damn you. People – and not just in the party – love to think the worst.

'Was it Rosa who added me to a list of suspected informers?'

'No, I don't think so. But who knows? Who cares?'

'She gave me a picture of her cat. You don't think that's odd?'

Koba shrugs. 'People like cats. They worship their cats – give them everything they can even when they have nothing themselves, and meanwhile their cats feel nothing but contempt in return. The relationship between a cat and their supposed owner is like the relationship between an emperor and the people.'

Elli turns to him and smiles. That face. He takes a breath. Looks away. Looks to where his father and that kid Gotsridze stand.

Spite, he thinks. Spite put Elli on that list. They knew he liked her, so they thought they'd take her away from him. Very simple. People underestimate the power of spite.

'But you're obligated now,' Elli says. 'They've done you a favour and you'll be expected to return it. You're comprom-ised. They'll hold it over you. Use it to keep you docile.'

'They might try. It's certainly a possibility.'

'They'll make you stop the expropriations.'

'They might try to do that too.'

'Promise me you won't.'

He says nothing. They both know a promise on its own is worthless. It's a loan that is not backed by collateral. A promise is like physical beauty, an asset whose value declines fast. A currency not worth investing in.

'I wish you'd let me see Tskhakaya.'

'Why? What did you want to say to him?'

'I didn't want to say anything. I wanted to shoot him.' She sighs now. 'It doesn't matter. I'm still here. The misunderstanding, whatever it was, has been cleared up and we can all think about more important things. But thank you. Even if it does mean I have the embarrassment of being saved by Mensheviks. And not just any Mensheviks. Julius Martov himself! We both have the shame of being in his debt. Like Adam and Eve being in the debt of the snake.'

'Like God himself being in the debt of the snake,' he says. Then, 'Do you have a gun?'

She shows him. Nina's gun, taken from her trunk while she was out with her footman.

He takes it from her. It's loaded.

'A Greener. Nice.'

'I was going to make him kneel down. I was going to make him take the gun in his mouth and then I was going to squeeze the trigger. I was going to do to him exactly what he wanted to do to me.' She sighs. 'I don't feel like doing that now. A shame that anger is so fleeting an emotion, something so hard to hold on to.'

Koba says nothing. He doesn't agree. He finds it easy to hold on to anger.

He points the gun in the direction of the grinning doltish faces of his father and Gotsridze. He fires. The report of the pistol reverberates around the park; a child cries, a man yells an oath, some of the rough sleepers stir, some of the amorous couples pause in their strokings and their rummagings, but

221

no one seems too bothered. He fires again. The idiot ghosts are unmoved, their rictus smiles as broad as ever, but now more people make the effort to be agitated. Some of the men struggle to their feet, bellow threats and imprecations towards where Koba and Elli sit.

'We'd best be off,' Koba says.

Elli is already standing. He hands her the gun.

A few minutes later, on another bench in another meagre park where there are more couples groping, more homeless men sleeping. Both of them are out of breath from the hardest running she's done since she can remember. Elli laughs, puts both her arms around Koba's shoulders. The gesture is affectionate. There's no heat in it. She smooths his unruly poet's hair.

'Oh, Koba,' she says, after a while. 'What will become of us?'

He thinks. He feels a buoyancy in his heart. In a few days, when Tskhakaya has recovered, he will be at the quayside in Harwich – pronounced *Harridge*. He will tip the porter that stows their cases too much money and he won't care about it. Shaumian and Tskhakaya will catch one ship and Koba will catch another. He will be alone on the boat to Hamburg and then the long train journey to Berlin.

He will be free for the first time in weeks. Maybe alone in his small cabin he will be able to finish another letter to Kato. Maybe, alone in his cabin, in peace, with nothing but the sound of water lapping against the sides of the boat, he'll be able to conjure up her face at least.

During these long weeks in Europe her features have been softening and blurring in his mind.

After this maybe he will drink and swap jokes with the commercial travellers and the German waiters returning home. He'll see his father of course and poor Gotsridze, but he will ignore them. Ghosts or phantasms conjured by his own mind, it doesn't matter – just two spirits, nowhere near enough to hurt. On the boat to Germany there will be drink and there will be singing and it will be enough to allow him to discount a couple of sullen dead faces for a while.

For a while too he will forget the existence of the Okhrana. He might even begin to forget Elli Vuokko.

Then there will be plans to make, actions to take, but their shape is uncertain. He can see as far as the Tiflis bank raid; after that everything is shrouded in mist and fog.

'Well, no ideas?' says Elli.

'The Tsar, encouraged by his generals, will embark on some foolish foreign adventure,' says Koba. 'Some Imperialist war which he'll lose. The people, angered by the cost of that war in lives and in treasure, by the fact that they are starving, that their oxen and their horses are dying in the fields, they will rise up. Martov and Plekhanov and the others of their kind will try to hold them back. Will try and say the people's demands should be reasonable, that they should stick to asking for one good meal a day. But the people won't be held back. They'll want everything. They'll want to burn everything down and then dance in the embers. We'll step in to direct the energy of the peasants. We'll remove the cowards and put the workers in charge of their destiny.'

'That simple?'

'That simple.'

'Didn't happen two years ago when the Tsar lost his war with Japan.'

'1915 won't be 1905.'

'You're a soothsayer today. What does your crystal ball

say about us, about Koba in Georgia and Elli Vuokko in Tampere?'

'We don't matter,' he says.

'We are nothing,' she says. 'But guess anyway. Use your imagination.'

'I can't,' he says. 'I have no imagination.'

'That's not true.'

It isn't true. He can imagine the future. He can imagine it very clearly. See exactly how it will be. He can feel it. Taste it. There will be growing numbers of the dead crowding in on him killing his rest, staring at him in parks like this in numbers he can't ignore and then, one day, when he is too exhausted to properly look out for himself, there will be the hot stab of a bullet between the shoulder blades, the twist of a knife in his guts, the scratch of the rope around his neck, the warm blood in his mouth. Koba himself ending as a ghost, haunting the dreams of Yakov, robbing the boy of his sleep, making him scared of the dark.

He forces himself to smile at her.

'After the revolution I will retire from politics. I will run a small bookshop in Gori,' he says. 'And you?'

'I will manage the factory where I currently work, because after the revolution female managers will be a normal thing. It won't even be commented on. And in my spare time I will take lovers. Lots of them. Good-looking men who can make me laugh. Older ones at first, men who I can teach about life. About the way things are. Then ones my own age. Then younger ones, they'll be the ones who can teach me. I have it all worked out.'

He laughs. The future she has mapped out for herself is clearly just as much of a lie as his own.

'No marriage? No children?'

'No marriage. No children. No cats even.'

They part as friends do. A chaste kiss on the cheek. A warm embrace. No tears.

They are, of course, both wrong. Koba will die in his bed at the age of seventy-three from a stroke. Elli Vuokko will be captured, raped then murdered by White Army soldiers at the age of thirty-one during the Finnish Civil War.

Hardly seems fair. He lives on forever. There are statues, monuments, museums. Her grave is unmarked. He haunts the dreams of millions. Her ghost appears to no one.

No-one forgets him; no one remembers her. Except us.

Author's Note

This story mixes historical characters and events with some that are invented. No apologies for this: all history is a construction and in a constant process of assembly, disassembly and re-assembly. Historical novels should not consist of a display of facts, however diligently excavated. However carefully polished and arranged. The French historical novelist Laurent Binet probably says it best in his great book *HHhH*: 'Fiction respects nothing'.

Nevertheless, the reader might find it helpful and interesting to have an outline of the specific events and characters that my novel is disrespecting.

Following abortive attempts to hold a conference in Norway then Denmark, the 5th Congress of the Russian Social Democratic Party did take place at the Brotherhood Church in Stepney from 11th May 1907. Stalin – then twenty-nine, a published poet, the man responsible for organising the bank robberies, or 'expropriations' that funded the Bolsheviks and calling himself Koba (after a Georgian folk-hero) – did attend as a non-voting delegate, as did Mikhail Tskhakaya and Stepan Shaumian. The argument about whether the Georgian Party was properly constituted was one of the first items of Congress business. It was Lenin's intervention that persuaded the Congress not to expel them.

Other leading communists who play a part in this story –

Trotsky (Yanofsky), Maxim Litvinov, Rosa Luxemburg, Mikhail Tskhakaya, Leo Jogiches, Maxim Gorky, Maria Andreyeva – all attended, as did others who are mentioned in passing. Luxemburg's and Jogiches' romantic relationship was falling apart, indeed was almost over, and Rosa Luxemburg really had begun a new partnership with Kostya Zetkin, the son of her friend Clara. Leo Jogiches was violently angry about this and threatened to kill either himself or Luxemburg. Rosa Luxemburg did stay at the Three Nuns Hotel when she first arrived in London for the Congress. All this is described in letters she wrote from London to Kostya, who stayed back in Berlin.

The female delegates – of which there were more than thirty – were offered martial arts training every morning before the Congress began, and these sessions were taken by Edith Garrud who also taught self-defence to the suffragettes.

Stalin and the other Georgians were staying at Tower House in Fieldgate Street (since demolished following bomb damage in World War 2) which was notoriously filthy. After one night they decamped to 77 Jubilee Street. It is not known exactly why they moved, though it is believed Stalin organised the change of address.

At Jubilee Street, Stalin did form an unlikely bond with a thirteen-year-old Arthur Bacon, who in 1950 allowed himself to be interviewed by the *London Evening News* on the subject of the 'Stalin I knew'. It's in this article that he reveals Stalin's taste for English sweets and the fact that he overcharged for any errands that he ran for the future Soviet leader. In this article he also reveals that he has become a Conservative supporter.

The delegates to the Congress did register at the Polish Workers Club, where they all took aliases and were allocated the passwords for the week. The building remains, though when I last went to London – in early 2020 – it had become a snooker hall.

The Congress attracted a great deal of attention from the tabloid press, especially from the relatively new *Daily Mirror*, which had been founded in 1905 as a paper for women. This approach of targeting female readers had not been as profitable as the owners had hoped and it had rebranded in an effort to take on the older *Daily Express*, running more political stories. News from the RSDLP Congress appeared in its pages every day that the delegates were in London.

It is in the *Daily Mirror* of 11th May 1907 that we can read about an eighteen-year-old female delegate with hair in a long plait down her back practising with a firearm. The report of the fiery speech of the Girl Nihilist is also from the *Daily Mirror*.

The idea of a professional secret police was a new one at this time. The Tsarist intelligence agency, the Okhrana, was one of the best funded. Their use of female agents, double agents and agents provocateurs to commit extreme acts of outrage that could be blamed on Leftists was well known.

The British Secret Service wasn't set up until 1909. Prior to that, intelligence gathering on potential enemies of the United Kingdom was the responsibility of MO3, a department of the Metropolitan Police which, for arcane bureaucratic reasons, was renamed MO5 in 1907. From the beginning there were accusations of collusion between British and Russian intelligence. While the Congress was ongoing, questions were asked in Parliament about the extent to which British agents were sharing information with the Tsar's secret police.

Rumours that Stalin had been an Okhrana agent began early in his career, and the fact that many of those who might have known the truth were later killed by him has done little to refute these insinuations. According to Roman Brackman's book *The Secret Life of Stalin* (Frank Cass, London, 2001) the young Josef Jughashvili was recruited around 1901, following a rogue agent provocateur operation in Tiflis, now Tblisi.

There was a historical Elli Vuokko, who fought for the Red Army in Finland's civil war and was killed as part of a White Army massacre in 1918. She may not have been a lathe operator, though female organisers in Finnish labour weren't unknown and most of the women soldiers serving on the frontline were from the young working class. I have borrowed her name and her age and tried to put her near the centre of the story as a way of making up for the way she, and many others like her, have been marginalised and forgotten.

There is no record of Stalin becoming romantically involved with anyone at this Congress, but we do know that he determinedly pursued younger women for much of his life regardless of his marital status.

His first wife Kato died of tuberculosis within six months of the end of the Congress. His son Yakov was raised by her family.

In truth we don't know much about what Stalin got up to in London. He wrote an article or two about the arguments with the Mensheviks that took place there (some of the content of which is used in this book as part of Elli Vuokko's speech towards the end of the opening day of the Congress), but beyond this he seems to have taken a deliberately low-key role.

We do know that the Bolsheviks ran out of money and

couldn't afford to get their delegates home until they had negotiated a loan from the philanthropist Joseph Fels. We also know that Stalin stayed in London later than the other delegates to nurse Mikhail Tskhakaya through a bout of severe influenza.

A few weeks after the end of the London Congress one of the world's most infamous bank robberies took place in Tiflis when, in a raid planned by Stalin, Lenin, Litvinov and others, Bolsheviks attacked the national bank in Tiflis. This robbery took place almost exactly as Koba describes it to Arthur.

These are the foundations on which I built this book and, I admit it, there are errors of fact. Some of them intentional. As the philosopher and novelist George Santayana wrote:

'History is a pack of lies about events that never happened told by people who weren't there.'

Acknowledgements

Thanks to the team at Sandstone Press – Robert Davidson, Moira Forsyth, Sue Foot, Ceris Jones, Alice Hamilton-Cox, Nicola Torch – and, especially, the incisive, forthright and sharp-eyed Kay Farrell who was most responsible for helping shape this book. Thanks are due too to Caron May for her usual tolerance as I locked myself away with Stalin, when we could have been doing stuff that was more obviously fun.

I'd also like to thank Herbie May, Hannah Procter, Joe Compton, Nicola Hogg, Duncan May, Carole May, Tony Cropper and Janet Cropper for their interest and support during the writing of this book. And a big hello to Nile Spark. Thanks too to Dr Jim English who made some telling observations and important suggestions. I'd also like to thank the Society of Authors, Arts Council England and the Arvon Foundation. All of them vital lifelines (lifeboats? lifebelts?) to many writers and to me in particular.

www.sandstonepress.com

Subscribe to our weekly newsletter for events information, author news, paperback and e-book deals, and the occasional photo of authors' pets!
bit.ly/SandstonePress

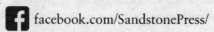 facebook.com/SandstonePress/

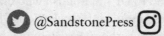 @SandstonePress